"Down!" Longarm barked.

He dropped to his belly, Colt in hand, as a second gunshot snapped through the broken window and again ricocheted dangerously off the cell bars.

Longarm fired blindly back into the new-fallen darkness. He had no target to aim at, no hope whatsoever that his slug would find a mark. He only wanted to give the sharpshooter pause.

A third incoming bullet tore splinters of wood out of the window frame and thumped into the wall behind Longarm.

A fourth bullet ripped through the window, higher this time, taking out what was left of the glass and spraying half the room with tiny shards.

Longarm felt one of them slice into his right cheek. Another nicked his ear.

If this kept up . . .

TABOR EVANS

LONGARM

ON THE
THUNDERBIRD RUN

J

JOVE BOOKS, NEW YORK

LONGARM ON THE THUNDERBIRD RUN

A Jove Book / published by arrangement with
the author

PRINTING HISTORY
Jove edition / March 1988

ISBN: 0-515-09491-9

Chapter 1

Longarm knocked on the door, the rap polite but firm, and took a step to the side. He really did not expect any trouble here, not this visit anyway, but a man never knew when some idiot with more brass than good sense might take a notion to slam a door into a man's face and come out with unpleasant intent. There was no point in taking chances, so he stepped aside to where a suddenly swinging door would pivot harmlessly away from him.

"Just a minute," a voice called from inside the sprawling, handsome house. It was a woman's voice.

Longarm removed his Stetson and stood, hat in hand, patiently waiting. He looked around the spread. Hell of a nice place, really. The outbuildings were as handsome as the house, everything large and nicely planned and kept in a state of fine repair. Well, they'd said at Snake Creek that Morey Fahnwell was the honcho of this country and damn near everything that adjoined it. God-awful rich was the way they'd actually put it. Longarm could believe it from looking at the Fahnwell headquarters.

On the other hand, Longarm had met many a wealthy old-timer who was content to live in a hole in the ground and walk around dressed like he couldn't afford a pot to spit in nor chew to work up the spit if someone would loan him the cuspidor. Fahnwell sure wasn't in that category.

"I'm coming," the harried-sounding female called again. "Really. Be right with you."

"Yes, ma'am," Longarm called back.

1

He looked around again, admiring the sound breeding he could see in the saddle horses being held in one of the many tightly built corrals and pens that surrounded the headquarters. The beeve he had seen on the ride in were every bit as fine-blooded as the Fahnwell horses. It was an impressive outfit.

But then it had every right to be, when you considered that all the grazing that put meat on the bones of those excellent horses and stocky, wide-bodied steers was coming to Fahnwell for nothing.

That was what brought Deputy United States Marshal Custis Long to the gentleman's door. The man had been grazing his beeve all to hell and gone across chunks of Wyoming, Utah, and Idaho—from Bear Lake to Green River and who knew how far from north to south—and he hadn't ever given in to the notion that the government was entitled to collect any grazing fees on all that government land.

Longarm's orders were to give Morey Fahnwell a not particularly subtle reminder about the oversight.

He heard a rapid-fire *tock-a-tock* approach of footsteps from the other side of the door, and the thing was pulled open by a breathless, harried-looking young woman. Her hair was coming down in rather fetching wisps from what was supposed to be a demure bun, and her cheeks were flushed. Perspiration showed on her forehead.

Those things probably should have been regarded as faults, but damned if Longarm could fault the pretty thing any other way.

My oh my, but she was something to look at.

Not a day over twenty, he would have wagered. Fresh and young and lovely. Slim as a reed except for a most appealing swell of breast and hip. Just about right for an armful. Light brown hair. Large, clear brown eyes. Mmmm.

Longarm smiled and stood tall. He had good enough reason to believe that he was not considered homely by very many available women. He was something over six feet tall, with a horseman's lean build and good shoulders. He had brown hair and a sweep of mustache against a face deeply tanned by years in the open. His eyes were brown, a touch darker than this girl's, and he affected clothing a cut above that worn by the cowboys this girl would mostly see.

"I'm sorry to take so long," she said, trying to control her breathing. Longarm did not mind her present condition, actually. The heaving for breath caused her chest to rise and fall and seemed to emphasize her considerable attributes.

"I have a pie in the oven, you see. It's a special pie. A birthday treat. And I am such a *terrible* cook at the best of times. And it was starting to burn. And then you knocked. And . . ."

He grinned at her. "Calm down. It's all right, miss. Did you get to that pie in time? I wouldn't want to ruin a birthday present."

"What? Oh, yes. It's on the rack now. I think it's all right." She fluttered her hands nervously, then took a deep breath and held it for a moment before puffing out her cheeks and exhaling slowly. When she had done that she seemed to feel better. She smiled at him.

My oh my, but she was a pretty one.

"Shall we start over?" she said graciously.

Longarm laughed. He made a shallow bow in her direction. "My name is Long, miss. And this, I take it, is the Fahnwell place?"

"That's right. I am Eugenie Fahnwell." She opened the door wider and stepped aside so he could come in.

"Then I'd guess it's your father I need to see, Miss Fahnwell."

Eugenie laughed gaily.

"Did I say something untoward, miss?"

"No," she said, still laughing. "You certainly aren't from around here, though, are you?"

"I'm from Denver," he admitted.

Smiling, Eugenie Fahnwell explained. "My father, Mr. Long, is in San Francisco to the best of my knowledge. He

3

is in business there. My *husband* will return with the rest of the men around sundown."

She seemed to thoroughly enjoy the look on Longarm's face.

"I shouldn't do that to perfectly innocent strangers. I do know better, Mr. Long. Truly I do. But sometimes I simply can't resist. And you really should have seen the utterly *horrified* expression you got. It was priceless. My apologies for enjoying your discomfort, sir." She giggled a bit, sounding not at all apologetic.

Longarm smiled at her. "I had heard that your husband was an elderly gentleman," he confessed.

"Oh, I shouldn't say elderly, Mr. Long. He is only sixty-four. And in an excellent state of health." She said that with a certain hint of relish that was enough to make Longarm feel damned well jealous of any sixty-four-year-old man—hell, face it, of anyone, any age—who could woo, win, and so obviously satisfy a filly like this one.

"I didn't mean . . ."

Mrs. Eugenie Fahnwell laughed again. "Of course you didn't. Forgive me for being such a tease."

Longarm was feeling damn well flustered. This self-possessed young woman was more than just an armful. There was a hell of a lot of female person hiding behind those pretty eyes and that dimpled smile.

"Come along, Mr. Long. You can help me decide if that pie looks nice enough for the table, and we can have a cup of tea while we wait for Morey."

"Yes, ma'am," Longarm said meekly. He trailed behind Mrs. Fahnwell while she strode briskly toward the back of the house, not at all breathless any longer and very much in control of the situation.

Chapter 2

United States Marshal William Vail stopped in midsentence and looked toward his office door as his clerk barged in without pausing to knock first.

Vail was busy, interviewing a job applicant, and Henry knew it. Even if no one had been in with the marshal, though, it was most unlike Henry to enter without permission.

"Yes, Henry?"

The clerk, whose meek appearance belied his courage, pushed his spectacles higher on the bridge of his nose in a nervous gesture, coughed politely into his fist, and then approached Vail's desk with a hurried apology. "I'm sorry to bust in on you like this, boss, but I thought you'd want to see this right away." He held out a flimsy sheet of yellow paper for Vail to take. "A messenger just now brought it."

The marshal for the Justice Department, Denver District, took the telegraph message form and shot a glance toward the visitor who wanted to become one of his deputies. "If you would excuse me for a moment?"

"Sure." The man made a show of peering at his fingernails, at a framed certificate on the office wall, and at almost everything else except Billy Vail and Henry.

Vail paused for a moment before he looked down at the message that Henry thought so important.

The job applicant, poor man, honestly did not realize that he had no chance of finding employment here. He was short and tubby—no harm in that, of course. Vail himself was none too much for height and his waistline had expanded since the years when he served in the field, first as a Texas Ranger, and then later as a deputy marshal himself. But the applicant had a look about him that said he was soft, too. Oh, he thought himself rugged enough for the job, that self-opinion based on eight months' service as a railroad detective. Billy Vail was not fooled, though. The man simply did not have what it took to be a federal deputy. Vail could see it in the man's eyes and hear it in the undertones beneath the blustering, frequently bragging voice. The marshal was only finishing out the interview as a politeness. He had no intention of hiring this one, even if they were shorthanded at the moment.

"Um. Yes. With you in a moment." Vail ignored both the applicant and Henry and concentrated on the telegram.

He read it through, double-checked the signature at the bottom, and read it through again.

"Damn!" he exclaimed.

"I thought you'd want to know right away," Henry said.

"Yes. You did the right thing. Thanks."

Henry remained standing by the desk, waiting for instructions.

Vail, although he knew perfectly well what the date was, checked the calendar on his desk and swore again. "We don't have much time, Henry."

"Three days," Henry confirmed.

"Where is—"

"Vacation," Henry responded quickly. "He never said where we could contact him."

"Smiley?"

"He's already left, boss."

"You're sure?"

Henry nodded. "He came by last night to pick up his travel vouchers. I happened to be here, finishing up some work after hours. He stopped in, oh, after nine it would've been." It was common enough for faithful Henry to stay late into the night when there was paperwork to be

6

completed. Vail knew that and appreciated the man's dedication, even if he seldom said so. "He said he would be taking a train out at first light."

"Did he say which line? We might be able to wire ahead and intercept him somewhere?"

"No, he didn't. He's on his way down to Durango to meet Dutch, and could be taking any of three rail lines out of Denver. Half a dozen different stage connections he might be thinking of making to get there. Smiley's out. So is Dutch, for that matter. I don't think we could get him up to Idaho in time, even if there was a telephone connection to Durango and you could talk to him right now."

"Damn," Vail muttered again.

"I could go," the interviewee said hopefully. "Whatever it is, Marshal, I could handle it."

Vail ignored him. So did Henry. If the marshal was not interested in accepting that offer, his clerk damn sure was not going to put an oar into the water.

"Long isn't too far away," Henry suggested. "We might be able to catch him with a wire to the sheriff at Snake Creek."

"And we might *not* catch him there," Billy Vail mused aloud. "If we miss him at Snake Creek . . ."

"He's the closest man we have. It's worth trying."

"But if we don't reach him?"

"Boss, Longarm is just about the *only* chance we have to nip this thing before it happens. We just don't have anyone else."

"Damn. Damn, damn, damnit! I'd go myself except that senatorial delegation is due in town tomorrow. The attorney general has already made it clear what is at stake there. If I don't show to hold their damn hands we could lose half our appropriation for next year. Senator Charlesworth gets his feelings hurt awfully easily, they say." Basically he was just thinking aloud, and Henry knew it.

"I could go," the job applicant said again. "Honestly, boss, I could handle it."

This time, at the man's presumption in the use of "boss," Vail scowled, effectively shutting the fellow up.

Vail looked down toward the telegram again.

INFORMATION FROM PRISONER WALDO STONE RE FORMER WHITE HOOD GANG INDICATES IMPENDING PAYROLL ROBBERY THIS FRIDAY AT THUNDERBIRD MINE COMMA THUNDERBIRD CANYON COMMA IDAHO STOP TRAIN HIJACK PLANNED BY SURVIVING GANG MEMBERS STOP STONE EXCHANGES INFORMATION FOR GOOD BEHAVIOR PAROLE RECOMMENDATION STOP SAYS MAIL CAR COMMA THUNDERBIRD CANYON NARROW GAUGE LINE COMMA TO BE HIT AT THUNDERBIRD TERMINUS STOP SCHEDULED ARRIVAL IS MIDAFTERNOON FRIDAY STOP MY BELIEF THIS FALLS UNDER YOUR JURISDICTION STOP FURTHER INFORMATION WILL FOLLOW IF AVAILABLE STOP SIGNED JOHNSON COMMA WARDEN COMMA FORT SMITH DETENTION

"Damn," Billy Vail said yet again.

"I already checked the map, boss. Thunderbird Canyon is—"

"Oh, I know where it is, Henry. I was there once, as a matter of fact. It's a silver-mining camp way the hell and gone back in the mountains on the Idaho side of the Idaho–Wyoming border country. There wasn't any railroad when I was there, though. Just the damnedest eyelash trail you ever saw. Everything had to move by mule then, in or out. The trail was too poor to trust a horse on, and even the mules lost footing now and then." Vail shook his head. He was still thinking aloud, and Henry kept his mouth shut while the boss pondered the problem.

A payroll was going to be lifted from a mail car under the protection of the U.S. government, and because of the short manpower of the moment and the poor transportation facilities, it looked like Billy Vail might have foreknowledge of a planned crime and yet be unable to do a damn thing about it.

"There is some local law there," Henry suggested. "I looked it up."

"Who?" There was eagerness in Billy Vail's voice. It was unusual for the federal government to appeal to local authority for assistance, but it was certainly not unheard of. Vail looked like he was willing to grasp at a straw if that was all he had to cling to on this one.

Henry pulled a note out of his pocket and glanced at it. "The sheriff's name is Markham. Paul S. Markham."

Vail rolled his eyes. "Damnit, Henry."

"Something wrong, boss?"

"Do you know Paul Sebastian Markham?"

"Never heard of him."

"Well, I wish I could say as much."

"A bad one, boss?"

"What? Oh." Vail sighed heavily. "No, Henry, Paul isn't a bad apple, if that's what you mean. He's honest enough. The poor man's just incompetent. Not his fault, of course. He just doesn't have it." Without saying it aloud Vail noted to himself that Paul Markham was very much like Vail expected this job applicant to be. Full of himself and a blusterer and undernourished in the brainpower department.

"We could go ahead and send a warning to him for whatever good it might do."

Vail sat back and rubbed a palm over his balding scalp while he stared at the ceiling and pondered. "Yes, we'll have to do that, of course. And try to contact Longarm. If we get lucky we might catch him at Snake Creek. He's close enough he could reach Thunderbird Canyon by Friday. If we get the message to him in time. If." He sighed again. "If it wasn't for that damned delegation of senators. . . . "

"I'll get the wires off right away to Sheriff Markham and to Longarm," Henry said. "And if you like, boss, I can draw a weapon and get on a train myself. I could make connections from here. Through Cheyenne and South Pass. You could give me a temporary commission easily enough. We've had to do it before, you know." Henry smiled gently.

Vail looked at the mild-seeming little man and smiled back at him. Yes, he remembered several such occasions from the past. Everything Henry did he did gently. But he was tenacious and honest and decent. He drew a clerk's meager salary, but that never stopped him from volunteering for hazardous duty when the need arose.

"If you left right now, Henry, you might not be able to make coach connections between the rails."

"And if I sit here in Denver we know I won't make those connections. I'm willing to give it a try, boss." Henry smiled. "After getting those wires off to Longarm and Sheriff Markham, that is."

"That would give us three chances at being there ahead of the robbers and being able to stop them."

"Three outside chances," Henry said, openly admitting what Billy Vail had been reluctant to state so bluntly. "Why, hell, boss, one of those long shots might pay off."

"I won't order you to go, Henry. You know that."

"If I remember correctly, boss, I went and volunteered."

The job applicant seated in front of Billy Vail's desk looked sourly from one man to the other. Billy Vail noticed the sudden change of expression and realized that before sundown the man would be making the rounds of Denver's saloons, bitching and moaning about what an unfair son of a bitch Billy Vail was. Probably a *stupid,* unfair son of a bitch after enough liquor passed the man's lips. No matter. Vail could live with an awful lot of that sort of thing. What he could not comfortably live with was the idea that a gang could hold up a mail car and him not be able to do anything about it even with advance knowledge of the gang's plan.

"Look here, Henry. Get those wires off right away. Warning messages to Markham and Long plus duplicates of this message from this Johnston fellow down at Fort Smith. And I suggest you carry along the Waldo Stone file.

It could come in handy if you and Longarm both get to Thunderbird Canyon ahead of the gang. I . . . can't think of anything else. You just have time enough to pack and get out to the depot for the Julesburg run as it is. If I think of anything else, I'll wire ahead and catch you at Cheyenne. You can check the telegraph office there. The U.P. always has a fairly lengthy stop there."

"All right. Wish me luck, boss."

"I do, Henry. I damn sure do." But he was saying it to Henry's back as the slender clerk bolted for the door.

Billy Vail waited for a moment, then with another sigh turned back to the glowering interviewee. Both men knew by now, of course, that they were only going through the motions, but Vail would do what courtesy required. Even though his thoughts were many miles away in an isolated canyon deep in the mountains of Idaho.

Chapter 3

Longarm stood at the parlor window, his teacup forgotten on the low table nearby, and watched the Fahnwell crew ride in.

He had no trouble picking out the boss. Fahnwell was tall and well-muscled—no running to fat in this one—with a touch of steel gray in his hair and mustache. He had no foreman, Eugenie had said. Longarm could see why. This man needed no one else to boss his hands, and probably would not have accepted a foreman's advice or assistance if there had been such a position among the crew.

Morey Fahnwell was a rarity in this country, a genuine old-timer. According to what his wife had said during the afternoon of tea and mild flirtation, Fahnwell had come to the country before there was an Idaho or a Utah or a Wyoming—back when men came here not to raise cows but to trap beaver.

Of course, he had been past the prime days of the beaver trade. The European market for the furs had already fallen to pieces, and the old-time mountain men were drifting away to look for more profitable work.

That had not stopped Fahnwell from trying to live out a dream, however, and when he failed as a trapper—as he had to—he made the most of his limited experience in the mountains. He began by guiding parties of emigrants moving west to Oregon and California and Washington, taking his pay in cash when the clients had it, in sure-footed livestock when they did not.

Over a period of years he accumulated a hell of a size-able herd of cattle, and horses too. He grazed them every-where there was grass within a week's riding distance, treated and traded with the Bannocks when that was possi-ble, and fought with them when it was necessary.

His riding crew, Longarm saw, still reflected that readi-ness to reach for their rifles. The men were hard. Not gunslicks, certainly, but tough and damned well compe-tent. Longarm could see it in the way the men carried themselves. There was an easy assurance about them. Whatever came their way, they had seen it already and had handled it before. Fahnwell had that same air about him. The man had seen the elephant. If the critter ever scared him in the past, he had long since gotten over his fears. Now he—and his men—knew they could cope with what-ever came to them.

Longarm smiled to himself. From everything he saw and everything he had heard, he suspected he was going to like Morey Fahnwell. Pity each of them might have to bare his teeth and growl at the other.

"Is that Morey?" Eugenie asked from behind him. She had gone to the kitchen to see to dinner. No hired cooks on this spread. Everyone pulled his or her own weight—the owner's forty-years-younger bride included.

"Yes." Longarm turned and smiled at her. "Handsome man, your husband."

"Handsome is as handsome does, Mr. Long." She re-turned the smile brightly. "Morey is indeed a handsome man."

"And a fortunate one," he complimented.

She laughed—as sure of herself as her husband was of himself—and bent to pick up the tea tray. "Morey will be in as soon as he washes up, Mr. Long. Will you join him in a whiskey? He can't abide tea, you know. Which is part of the reason it's been such a pleasure for me to have your company this afternoon."

"A whiskey would be nice, ma'am. Rye if you have it."

"Of course. Rye is Morey's favorite too. He claims

bourbon is for . . . well, never mind *what* he says bourbon is for. I couldn't possibly repeat it."

Longarm laughed.

Eugenie Fahnwell poured two generous glasses of rye whiskey from a bottle of venerable age and outstanding experience, Longarm noted from the label. She set the first on a coaster beside a heavy, leather-covered armchair and ottoman that were probably even older than the whiskey and handed the other to Longarm.

The drinks were served just in time for Morey Fahnwell's arrival from the back of the house. The man bent to kiss his pretty wife and give her a playful squeeze—which Longarm pretended not to notice—then turned to their guest with a smile and an extended hand. "How d'you do, sir. I saw the horse outside. Livery mount from Snake Creek if I'm not mistaken, which makes you a stranger to the country. And that, of course, means that you've no table of your own handy. I hope Eugenie has invited you to dinner, sir."

Longarm grinned and shook the man's hand. "You do get right down to things, I see." He paused. "If the invitation stands later on, sir, I would be proud to have supper with you and the lady. Although with apologies. I didn't know it was your birthday, and of course if you would rather be alone . . ."

Fahnwell threw his head back and laughed. "The private celebratin' will come later." He winked at Longarm and put an arm affectionately over Eugenie's shoulders.

"My name is Long, Mr. Fahnwell. Custis Long of Denver."

"Of Denver, eh? It's a long way to come on business unstated, sir."

Damnit, Longarm *did* like this man—and Eugenie, too. Still, he was not much given to lying, and nothing would be gained by pretending to be something other than what he was.

"I'm a deputy United States marshal, Mr. Fahnwell, and

14

I've been asked to sit down with you and discuss recent oversights."

Longarm expected anger. Perhaps even rage from this proud and capable old man. Instead he got laughter.

Once again Morey Fahnwell threw his head back and roared with laughter. He laughed hard, then settled himself into his favorite armchair and raised his glass of rye in a silent salute to his guest. He drank off half the generous measure with pleasure, then smiled at Longarm. "Oversights," he said, mouthing the word as carefully as he had tasted the whiskey. "An interestingly delicate phrasing, Mr. Long. For Eugenie's benefit, sir?"

"Uh . . . yes, as a matter of fact."

Fahnwell chuckled and asked his wife to see to their supper. "Set the table for three please, Eugenie. We'll be in shortly."

"Yes, Morey." Longarm thought she looked a little worried when she left the room, but she did not question her husband's wishes. Hell of a woman, Longarm thought. For that matter, hell of a couple. He was beginning to wish that his business here was social.

When Eugenie was gone, Fahnwell motioned Longarm into the second most comfortable chair in the room and took another drink, this time sipping the rye slowly and savoring it.

"Come t' take me in in chains, young man?"

"Not if I can help it," Longarm answered truthfully. "Only if I have to."

Fahnwell gave him a quiet smile. "Might not be so easy, you know. If you decide you have to, that is."

Longarm smiled back at him and tasted the rye he had been served. It was every bit as good as he expected. Certainly better than anything he could afford on a government salary. "If a man asks for easy all his life, he won't have much of a life to take easy. Will he?"

Morey Fahnwell chuckled. "Nicely put, Mr. Long."

"Call me Longarm. All my friends do."

"Ah, an' you'd like us t' be friends, Mr. Long?"

"It isn't necessary, Mr. Fahnwell. And it won't change anything if it does become so. But, yes, I would like that."

"All right," Fahnwell said, grinning. "Longarm."

"You know what I've come about, Morey. I'd like to settle this in a friendly way."

For the first time Fahnwell's smile faded, and he looked serious. He also looked his age for the first time then, Longarm realized.

"Those red-tape bastards want to nickel an' dime a man to death, Longarm. You know that as well as I do. Who was it stood up to the Bannocks in the old days, Longarm? 'Twasn't any paper-shuffling son of a bitch in Washington, I can tell you that. It was me and my boys. We smelt smoke from the peace pipe and we smelt smoke from our rifles and we cut arrows outa young heifers and we went to bed every night not knowin' if we'd be alive to see the dawn. We done that, Longarm—not some damned thief in a government office. Now them bastards want me to pay for what God an' a Spencer repeating carbine made mine. They want me to pay for what's already mine, Longarm. I know you can understand that."

Longarm took another swallow of the excellent rye. "I won't argue the point with you, Morey. On a personal level, if it came to that, I'd probably have to agree with you. The point is, though, that like it or not, the law is the law. We live with the law or we move out beyond it. We don't have any other choices."

Fahnwell laughed again, but this time the sound of it was short and bitter. "I did that already. Problem is, the damned law caught up with me an' surrounded me. Worse damn ambush than any of the Injuns ever laid for me, I can tell you."

"You can fight a Bannock," Longarm agreed. "There's no way you can fight a bureaucrat."

"A man can always fight, Longarm."

"That kind of fight is for stupidity, not purpose," Longarm said softly over the rim of his glass. "A man doesn't build what you have here out of stupidity."

"But if I damn well choose to be stupid?"

Longarm shrugged.

"You'd shoot me down to take me in if you had to?"

"Over a couple dollars? Of course not, Morey."

"You're saying you wouldn't shoot me down then, Longarm? No matter what?"

It was Longarm's turn to laugh. "Now damnit, Morey, don't get so notional. I like you. But I don't like you or anybody else so much that I'm willing to make promises I might not be able to keep. I thought you were smart enough to know that."

Fahnwell's smile returned. "Yeah. So I do. Pity them fools back east don't understand the worth of a man's word. Me and the boys would've had less Injun trouble these years past if anybody back there understood what a man's word oughta mean."

Again Longarm could find no fault with the man's statement. He kept his silence and had another drink of the rye.

"Let's peg this in place, Longarm. Just so I know what my choices are. You say you didn't come here to drag me off in irons. What do you want?"

"I want you to ride into Snake Creek with me tomorrow morning. I want you to take that grazing fee out of the bank, pay it, and put the receipt in your pocket. Then I want you and me to have a drink together before you come back home and I go off to more important business than the collecting of a few cents per head for cows grazed on government-owned lands." He took another drink. "That's what I'd like, Morey."

"Do you know how many cows I got on that so-called government land, Longarm?"

"I got no idea, Morey. Hell, I'd bet you don't know exactly how many there are. The bureaucrats claim you're running four thousand head on public land. That's the number they want to collect on and that's the number I want you to pay on."

Fahnwell was almost able to hide the laughter that was rolling inside his belly. Longarm was willing to bet that the

17

old man was running five, maybe ten times that number of beeve on public land.

"Damnit, Morey, if you up and volunteer to pay double what they want, you'd still be getting a hell of a bargain."

"It'd still be paying for what I already own," Fahnwell insisted.

"We both know better, Morey. It's land you civilized, sure, but it isn't land you own. Not under the law, you don't."

"And that right there is the quarrel between you and me, Longarm."

"Doesn't have to be any quarrel between us, Morey. That's what I'm trying to say here."

"An' if I don't roll over and yip for them sons of bitches, Longarm?"

"Bureaucrats always win, Morey. In the long run they just naturally do. They're thick-skinned and thick-headed and they just don't care about right or wrong. They only care about law. You can fight them, but you can't beat them. Better to pity the bastards their ignorance than to fight somebody you'll never even see, much less back down."

"So if I refuse to knuckle under, it comes down to a war between you and me, Longarm?"

"No, Morey. I won't fight you that way. Not even if you try and push me into it for some crazy, grandiose gesture that'd only end with everybody getting hurt one way or another."

"You ain't going to arrest me; you ain't going to shoot me; you say you ain't even going to fight me, Longarm. Just what do you figure to do if we don't take that ride to town tomorra?"

"I don't want to sound like I'm making threats, Morey. I didn't come here to threaten you either."

"Damn, but you're a hard man to pin down, Longarm. So all right. You aren't threatening. I'm asking. Would you please tell me?"

Longarm shrugged again. "I've given it some thought

this afternoon, I grant you. What I decided was that if you don't want to pay the pittance to the fools back east, I'll wander over to Fort Washakie. They got a bunch of under-employed troopers over there with no Indians to fight at the moment. I expect they need something to do. So I guess I'd go round up a couple troops of cavalry and put them to work keeping your cows on your deeded acreage and off the government land. I expect that many cows could manage for a time on the land you do own, and everything would be nice and legal that way, nobody hurt. Of course, it's always possible that some of them troopers can count. If they turn up with twenty or thirty thousand head of livestock where the paper shufflers thought there were only four thousand, well, word of it could get back to Washington. That'd be a shame. Then those silly bastards would be dunning you for a whole lot more than a few hundred dollars they want as it is." He swallowed off the last of his whiskey. "Mind if I smoke in here, or should I go out on the porch?"

"You son of a bitch."

Longarm looked up. Morey Fahnwell was laughing again, his belly shaking with it. Longarm grinned at him.

"You do reach for the short hairs, don't you?"

"Just trying to be fair and reasonable, Morey."

"By God, Longarm, it's lucky for people like me that those idiots in Washington aren't your kind of fair an' reasonable." Fahnwell stood. "Let me refill these glasses an' then we'll go out to the porch for a smoke before dinner."

It was after dinner. The meal was long on quantity but otherwise perfectly horrid; Eugenie had not been fibbing about her deficiencies in the kitchen.

The three of them were seated in caneback rockers on the porch enjoying the evening air, Longarm and Morey Fahnwell with drinks and cigars while Eugenie had a cup of tea.

"Longarm will be staying the night with us, dear," Morey said.

"I'll air out the guest room for him then."

"You do that. Then come morning the two of us will be riding to town. We have some business there." He winked at Longarm but did not explain. "Mind you, take a minute before we go up to bed. Make up a list of anything you need from town. Or come with us if you'd rather. I'm sure Longarm wouldn't mind company other than mine."

"It will be a pleasure," Longarm said seriously. "I expect to have good company either way."

Fahnwell threw his head back and laughed. Eugenie, though obviously uncertain about what all had gone on between these two men, smiled. She stood. "If you would excuse me then, I shall see to your room, Mr. Long."

"And I'll go inside an' fetch out that bottle. I think you and me could do some drinking together t'night, Longarm."

"My pleasure, Morey," Longarm said. He meant it.

Chapter 4

Henry swung down to the depot platform even before the chuffing, clanking freight came to a complete halt. He was feeling anxious, worried. The damned trip was moving so *slowly*. Typical when a man was in a great hurry, of course. But this was ridiculous.

In order to get west, out in Idaho, he had been required first to travel east. Out the branch line from Denver to Julesburg, then a seemingly interminable wait there for a westbound night freight, and now finally to Cheyenne on the Union Pacific main line.

He was beginning to feel like he would never be able to reach Thunderbird Canyon in time. And in truth, if he *did* get there in advance of the robbery deadline, he was still hoping with a powerful intensity that Longarm would receive the message and be there too. It was one thing to offer backup assistance to a deputy. It was quite something else to carry the weight of responsibility oneself for an entire case.

Henry had no delusions about himself. He believed in giving all he had to his responsibilities, but he did not fancy himself a hell-for-leather peace officer in clerk's guise. He *was* a clerk, damnit. A good one. The very best clerk he could possibly be. But he had no secret ambitions to replace Longarm or Dutch or any of these boys. Not really.

Lordy, but he hoped Custis would get there before him.

He clutched his grip in a sweaty hand—the borrowed

Colt revolver and a small, exceptionally heavy box of .45 caliber ammunition inside the bag were swaddled in his spare underclothing—and hurried to the end of the platform. The engine was still discharging its head of steam and the brakes were squealing their last protest against the inertia of the heavily laden freight cars.

It was not yet dawn, and the platform was empty. There were a few night lamps glowing inside the station, but no sign of people or movement save the crew of the train he had just been on and a single yawning workman.

Henry tried the door to the telegrapher's office and found it locked. He peered through the grimy glass window into the small, cluttered office. The telegrapher's desk was empty, his key silent.

"Damn," Henry muttered aloud.

He looked inside the depot waiting room, but the ticket window and dispatcher's station were dark and silent. Two lamps burned at either end of the long room, probably left for the convenience of would-be passengers waiting for morning connections. But there was no sign of life anywhere.

"Damn," he murmured again.

He set his bag by the telegraph office door and hurried down the platform, shoes crunching over the soot and clinkers left by the coal-fired engines and years of rail traffic, and accosted the lone workman who seemed to belong here.

"You!" Henry snapped, his voice taking on a rare note of authority.

The man blinked and peered at him but did not otherwise respond.

"I'm looking for the telegraph operator," Henry said. "Surely you have a night operator."

The man nodded mutely.

"Well?"

The laborer scratched an unshaven chin, thought about the question for a moment, and finally said, "Well what, mister?"

"The telegrapher. Where is he?"

The workman shrugged, thought again and ventured, "Could be over t' the crapper. Mebe havin' a cuppa coffee an' fresh cruller. Miz Jolene, she has her mornin' baking done 'bout now. Could be over there. I dunno, mister."

"I need to see him. Immediately. I want you to find him and bring him here at once," Henry ordered.

The workman looked Henry up and down and apparently was unimpressed by what he saw. The fellow was half a head taller and half again wider than clerkish Henry.

"Up yours, asshole. It ain't my job t' run errands fer the customers." He turned his attention back toward the engineer high in the cab of the huge locomotive.

Henry grabbed the insolent fellow by the elbow and spun him half around so that they were face to face. He pushed his nose directly under the workman's, having to come onto his tiptoes to do it, and snarled, "I am a deputy United States marshal, buster, and you won't *have* a job with this railroad past daybreak if you do not go *immediately* and fetch that telegraph operator to me. Right *now!*"

The man blinked again, rapidly, and pulled away.

Henry did not let it show, but his heart was beating at an unnatural pace. If this big son of a bitch refused . . .

"Now!" Henry snapped again.

"Uh . . . yes . . . uh, sir."

The burly workman actually knuckled his forehead before he turned and hurried away into the dark of the pre-dawn.

Henry let out a sigh of considerable relief. He also straightened his shoulders and puffed out his chest just a bit—once the workman was out of sight, that is.

He had gone and done it. Faced the fellow right down and told him what to do. And he was *doing* it. Why, that was something. That was really something.

Feeling suddenly powerful and peacock-proud, Henry marched himself back to the closed and locked telegraph office and stood before the door with his arms folded and a truculent expression on his face.

These people *would* perform as he required, by Godfrey, or he would know the reason why. And he *would* be on the next available westbound. Complete with any information Marshal Vail might have forwarded or any new instructions.

Yessir, by Godfrey, he was on a case and he would get done whatever had to be done. Regardless.

He smiled a little to himself and waited for the night telegrapher to return to his proper post.

Chapter 5

Morey Fahnwell accepted the thin sheaf of large, gold-backed bills and counted them carefully before he thanked the teller at the tiny bank. Then the man turned and extended them to Longarm, giving the deputy a wry grin. "There, damn you. One hundred sixty dollars legal tender. Every damn thing I owe on four thousand head at four cents apiece for your stinking damn totally unfair grazing fee."

Longarm laughed, but shook his head. "It isn't me you owe that money to, Morey. I just came to see it paid, not to handle it." The laughter turned into a grin. "Why, a poor, underpaid civil servant like me, seeing that kind of cash money in hand, I might get to thinking you were trying to bribe me, and have to arrest you for that. You know damn well where that money has to be paid, Morey."

Fahnwell grumbled and groused. "Damnit, Longarm, d'you know how I'll feel if I hafta walk into that office an' lay money in front of them? D'you know the kind of horselaugh I'll get?"

"Not till your back is turned, Morey," Longarm said cheerfully.

Fahnwell made a sour face. "You'll go with me at least, won't you? So them red-tape sons of bitches will know I was forced inta this?"

"Yeah, I can do that for you, Morey."

The old rancher grunted and grumbled some more. "Some damn friend you turn out t'be." But he left the bank and walked with Longarm down the street to the court-house.

"Just think, Morey," Longarm twitted him, "you're gonna have a warm feeling in your heart when this is done. Civic duty performed and all that."

"Damn you, boy, you better shut your mouth or I'll sull up like an old cow. Turn right around an' go home. Do somethin' *decent* with this here cash money. Like get drunk on it or blow it on foofaraw for Eugenie or something *sensible* like that."

He was just blowing smoke, and Longarm knew it. Longarm was stone-cold positive that once Morey Fahnwell could be convinced to give his word on a subject, that statement was worth more than many men's signed, sworn, and sealed contracts. The likable old curmudgeon was solid proud, right down to the core, and there wouldn't be any way Longarm could force him not to make the payment now that he had said he would pay the hated fees.

They climbed the steps of the native quarry-stone court-house building, and Longarm held the door open for the rancher to enter.

"Huh! 'Bout time I got some service outta the damn government."

Longarm chuckled and followed him inside.

"Quick as I get this misery over with, boy, we'll go have us a drink."

"Whose treat?" Longarm demanded.

"Boy, you don't give a man a damned inch, do you. All right, damnit, I'll even go that." Fahnwell was trying to look and sound ferocious, but there was a sparkle of rough pleasure in his eyes. He was enjoying Longarm's company as much as the tall deputy was enjoying his.

They were passing the county sheriff's office on their way to the curving staircase that led to the second floor. A young man inside who looked more like a store clerk than a deputy looked up and noticed them. Longarm nodded to him and went on by.

As they reached the foot of the staircase a voice behind them called out, "Excuse me."

Both men stopped and turned.

"Excuse me, please? Would you happen to be a Marshal Long?" It was the young deputy asking.

Longarm nodded. "I would."

The young man looked relieved. "Good. A message came for you last night, Marshal. Urgent. Sheriff Tate left word that we was to be looking for you."

"Urgent, you say?"

"That's right, Marshal."

Longarm gave Morey Fahnwell a look of apology and returned down the wide hallway to the sheriff's small office. Fahnwell mounted the stairs by himself to pay off the grazing fee obligation.

"The message is right here, Marshal," the local deputy said, digging through a stack of papers. "Right here someplace. Sure hope I haven't lost it."

Longarm curbed his impatience and pulled out a cheroot. Rushing the boy likely would not accomplish anything but to make him even more fumble-fingered.

"Take your time," he said, not meaning a word of it.

Billy Vail was not a man to mark a message urgent if there were not real need for urgency.

While the young deputy continued to shuffle through the papers, Longarm reflected that it was a damn good thing he had not had to ride for Fort Washakie this morning instead of Snake Creek. Billy never would have thought to look for him there.

"Ah. Here 'tis," the deputy said finally. He pulled out a pair of yellow message slips pinned together and handed them to the federal officer.

Chapter 6

Longarm extended his hand to Morey Fahnwell. "I'll have to hit you up for that drink another time."

"I understand," Morey said.

Longarm reached for the reins of his rented horse.

"Wait a second, boy."

"What is it, Morey? I haven't much time according to these telegrams."

"I know that, damnit. I'm not holding you here for the hell of it. You ever been to Thunderbird Canyon, Longarm?"

He shook his head.

"Well, I have. I sell beef there. Standing order each an' every month of the year, so I know something about that country."

Longarm quit fidgeting and paid attention. If Morey had something to say, perhaps he should listen to his advice. A man could get into too much of a hurry for his own good. "All right," Longarm said, "go ahead."

"First thing, you leave that nag be. I know that horse. It's a fair animal, but it ain't what you're needing today, my friend."

"But I don't—"

Fahnwell cut him off with an upraised hand. "Now you just hear me out for a minute here."

Longarm smiled at the old fellow and took out another cheroot, offering one to Morey as well.

"Thanks." Fahnwell bit off the twisted tip of the smoke

and bent to the match Longarm held in cupped hands. "Mmm. Not bad. I'll have to see if Sam can't stock some of these for me."

"Morey!" Longarm groaned, becoming exasperated again.

"Calm down, sonny boy. Calm down." Fahnwell winked at him, then continued. "The thing is, that there message of yours says the robbery's to take place Friday afternoon, mmm?"

Longarm nodded.

"This here's Wednesday. Doesn't give you a whole hell of a lot o' time to get there an' get yourself set."

"I know that, Morey. That's why..."

"Damnit, boy, you hush and listen to me. Like I told you, I do business in Thunderbird Canyon regular. Supply eatin' beef to the silver mines in that canyon an' to the butchershop, hotel, an' several outfits like that. So I know what I'm telling you. The only way into that canyon is by the railroad."

"The *only* way?"

"Did I say only? What I meant to say was *o-n-l-y* only. Used to be a pack trail. One hair raisin' son of a bitch it was, too. Hung onto a lip o' rock high on the canyon wall. Except it ain't there anymore. When they built the railroad, they had to go in over that same trail. It's the onliest way there is. O' course, once you're back in there you can reach the plateau up above the trail, climb up inta the mountains some, like that. But the onliest way in or out is by that train now that the trail is under steel rails. Which is part o' what I'm trying to tell you.

"That narrow-gauge line—and believe me, Longarm, it's the narrowest damn dinky little narrow-gauge thing I ever seen—don't run but twice a day. Once up, once down. South end, which is where you'll have to pick it up, is at Meade Park. That's about seventy-five miles north from here. You know the town?"

"I've heard of it. Never been there."

"All right then. You got to get to Meade Park, and you

got to do that before the afternoon upbound heads into the canyon. Otherwise you won't be going in at all before the train that's supposed t' be robbed. Now you see what I'm tryin' to tell you?"

"I'm commencing to," Longarm acknowledged.

"Exactly. You got seventy-five miles to go and"—Morey pulled out his watch and checked the time —"an' just under twenty-four hours to make the ride."

"Ouch," Longarm said.

"Ouch? You damn well betcha. That livery horse there won't begin to make that distance in less'n a day."

Longarm frowned. "That may well be, Morey, but I got to try. If I kill the son of a bitch I got to try. The White Hood outfit is a bad one. We've nibbled at the fringes of them, but this is the first chance we've ever had to really pin them to the wall. If there's any way at all—"

"Will you quit interrupting me, please?"

"Sorry."

"The point I been trying to get across to you, son, is that that livery nag you're on won't come close to making it to Meade Park in time. But this hammerheaded little snide of mine, well, it'd get you there with time t' spare."

Longarm looked at Morey Fahnwell's personal mount.

Hammerheaded little snide, the man had called it? Every horse on the Fahnwell ranch was about as good a quality mount as a man could ever hope to see. And this "snide" that Morey chose for himself was the best of the best. The horse was young, not more than five if that, and sleek as an otter. It had muscles that looked like rippling steel cable under a glossy chestnut hide, and its eyes were large and intelligent. It had wide flaring nostrils able to scoop in wind by the bucketful and a chest like a beer keg.

"Snide, huh?"

Morey grinned. "What I'm telling you, my friend, is that it'd be time well spent if you switched your saddle and gear to my ugly plug an' take it on the road to Meade Park. This youngun will put you there in plenty of time to catch the afternoon upbound, and you'll be layin' in position there long before your robber boys come to pay their call."

"It occurs to me," Longarm said, already reaching to unstrap the cinch of his McClellan from the livery horse, "that I'm becoming just as glad that I didn't have to shoot you yesterday."

Fahnwell laughed and began stripping his gear from the chestnut.

"I'll bring him back first chance I get. No guarantees when that will be." He pulled the cavalry saddle off the rented horse and smoothed his blanket over the back of the young chestnut.

"No hurry. If he don't come back at all, I'll understand. I'm not one to begrudge a friend a loan."

Longarm was in a hurry, but he couldn't help stopping what he was doing and turning to give Morey Fahnwell a stare and a laugh. "You old son of a bitch. D'you realize that this horse is probably worth more than the grazing fee you've been pissing and moaning about all this time?"

Morey grinned right back at him, quite unabashed. "Principle, son. If a man don't have principles, he don't have nothing."

Longarm clapped the man on the shoulder, switched his Spanish-bitted bridle to the tough chestnut and swung into the saddle. He reached down to shake Morey's hand. "Thanks. I'll get back when I can."

Fahnwell nodded and took a puff on the cheroot Longarm had given him. "Eugenie'll have supper on the table when you get there. And mind you, we'll be expecting you t' stay the night."

Longarm touched the brim of his Stetson in silent salute to the old man who was every bit as tough and rugged as this young horse of his. Then he touched his spurs to the flanks of the chestnut and put the horse into a lope toward the north.

This was going to be a long and tiresome ride.

Chapter 7

The sturdy chestnut—moving that afternoon and on through the night and following morning in the steady walk, trot, and lope rhythm of the long-distance cavalry march—put Longarm in Meade Park with hours to spare. The livery mount from Snake Creek, he was sure, would have died of exhaustion miles to the south, but the chestnut could have gone on another ten or fifteen miles if it had had to.

Tired as he was, the first thing Longarm did when he reached the town was find the livery.

"I need a stall," he told the hostler. "I want a box stall, and I want it bedded a good two feet deep with fresh straw."

"Are you crazy, mister? I don't—"

"You will this time," Longarm informed the man. He handed the fellow a five dollar half eagle. It was enough to pop the man's eyes and shut his mouth.

"Like I said," Longarm went on, "I want a box stall bedded two feet deep. And I want your bottle of whiskey. I expect you've got one tucked away someplace?"

"Ayuh, I might."

"Then drag it out here and get to forking fresh straw into that stall."

While the hostler cleaned and rebedded the best stall in the barn, Longarm poured half the bottle of whiskey into a bucket of water and used the alcohol and water mixture to give Morey Fahnwell's grand chestnut a thorough wash and rubdown, paying particular attention to the stout animal's legs and feet. Then he swabbed out its nostrils and mouth with the whiskey mix, but would not allow the horse to drink yet.

Part of the remainder of the liquor went into a thick mash of barley and bran for the chestnut to eat. A swallow or two went into Longarm's empty belly. There had been neither time nor place for him to eat since he left Snake Creek. But that could come later.

"What time is the train to Thunderbird Canyon?" he asked the hostler while he tended the horse.

"'Nuther hour," the man said.

"I'll be gone a day, maybe two. Until I get back, mister, I expect this little horse to be treated like a house pet. You understand me? The thing wants to sit in your lap and have you read to it of an evening, then that's what it gets. Right?"

"Well, I don't . . ."

"Five dollars a day for that kind of babying," Longarm said gently. "I'll pay it gladly. On the other hand, if I decide I'm not satisfied, I'll pull your tongue out and tie it around your neck like a kerchief. Do we understand each other?"

"Uh . . . yeah."

"Thank you, sir. That's mighty kind of you."

Longarm thoroughly bathed and rubbed the chestnut, saw that it ate greedily of the fortified mash, and only then allowed it a drink, the drinking water slightly fortified with the last of the whiskey.

"This horse has done a hell of a piece of work," Longarm told the hostler when he was ready to leave for the railroad depot. "You take care of it like I would, and there'll be a bonus in it for you when I get back. Otherwise . . ." He let the rest of it hang unspoken in the air. The hostler nodded solemnly and assured him the chestnut could sleep in his own bunk if the horse damn well felt like it.

"Good." Longarm left his saddle and bridle at the livery and carried the rest of his gear out into the street.

There was not a hell of a lot to see in Meade Park. It was a small town, a former mining camp gone once already to ruin, and now hanging on as the southern terminus of the narrow-gauge railroad that fed into Thunderbird Canyon. Even though the nearby mines Longarm could see were tumbledown and apparently abandoned, there was a stamp mill and refinery raising noise and smoke at the side of a brisk-running creek. Longarm guessed that silver ore from Thunderbird Canyon was hauled here for processing at the facilities already established when Meade Park was actively mining. That would be the reason for the railroad, he gathered.

Normal procedure would be for him to check in with the local law before going on to Thunderbird Canyon.

But he decided against that. The White Hood Gang was known for its swift and cleverly-planned strikes and ghost-like getaways. They were probably the most successful outfit operating in the past half dozen years, and he wanted to take them.

Damn, but he wanted to take them down.

Whoever they were, they were awfully good.

Far from the busiest robbery gang, they were without doubt the best. If anything failed to match up with their expectations they turned quietly away and disappeared. They had learned that much from Waldo Stone, who also tipped them to this job.

Stone's capture by Smiley several months back had been pure luck. Smiley had been fortunate enough to be in the vicinity when the White Hoods took more than $35,000 out of a bank in southern Utah. The only reason Stone had gotten inside Smiley's manacles was because the fleeing robber's horse took a spill, and Smiley was able to reach him before the rest of his crowd could come back to rescue him. Stone was bitter now because the outfit had not shot it out with Smiley. But one hell of a big posse was behind Smiley and riding hard at the time.

Now, by damn, Longarm had a chance at the rest of the crowd. He was not going to risk it by tipping the local law in Meade Park to the possibility of an ambush when the job came down.

No, sir, he was not.

The damned White Hoods were reputed to have their ears pressed to every wall. Their information was always good, their planning impeccable, and their execution faultless.

One whisper of warning reaching the wrong ear, and the bunch would disappear into the mountains without Longarm ever knowing who they were or where they had been.

Careful as the bastards were about their identities, he could sit next to one of them at a lunch counter and never know it.

So he was taking no chances this time.

At the rail depot he did not even use his pass to secure a seat on the northbound into the canyon. He pulled out cash and forked over the price of a ticket like any other passenger with business at the silver camp.

He bought his ticket with half an hour to spare and used the time to buy himself a box lunch to carry on the train, a pair of doughnuts that he wolfed down on the spot to take the edge off his hunger, and a cup of coffee strong enough to damn near wake him up.

Lordy, but he couldn't remember ever being so tired before. Worth it, though. If he could get a crack at the White Hoods, it would all be worth it.

He carried his box lunch and gear to a bench on the platform and slumped down onto it.

The train was already made up and building steam. The outfit—engine, wood car, one passenger coach, and a string of open-topped ore trucks—was the puniest damn thing Longarm had ever seen on actual rails. The locomotive didn't look much bigger than a toy engine.

That made sense, of course. There was no connecting line within fifty, sixty miles. The whole shebang, engine and all, would have to have been brought in piecemeal on mule packs or freight wagons and assembled here on the spot. And right now Longarm did not give a particular damn what the train looked like—just that the thing would get him up to Thunderbird Canyon ahead of the White Hoods.

Meantime all he wanted was to sleep. He let his eyes sag closed, and he drowsed while he waited for the conductor to call for boarding.

Chapter 8

The Thunderbird Run, which is what they called the single train that operated on the narrow-gauge line into Thunderbird Canyon, was set up oddly.

There was the toy box engine at the front, of course, followed by a tender stuffed with locally available wood rather than coal, then a crew car that looked like a miniature version of a caboose. Next came the string of open-topped ore cars, built with hopper sides so the silver ore could be readily unloaded at the Meade Park mill and refinery. Finally, like an afterthought, there was the lone passenger car tucked away at the tail end of the procession.

No diner or sleeper would be needed on the short run of the Thunderbird, naturally, but there was no smoker either. A platform on the back of the narrow passenger coach served that purpose when necessary, although the litter of pipe dottle and cigar butts on the coach floor showed that the one car was normally a smoker until or unless there were ladies present on the journey.

This trip, to Longarm's considerable disgust, there was a young woman in one of the seats, surrounded by three youngsters with bright eyes, slobbery grins, and loud mouths. With their yammering so close by Longarm could not sleep, and with the woman there he could not smoke. He was glad the trip was only supposed to take a couple hours.

He frowned and settled for going out onto the iron-rail-enclosed platform. In inclement weather the trip would be a torture with that family aboard.

"Howdy." He nodded to the other occupant of the platform, who had preceded him out of the noise of the coach.

"Hello." The man smiled and pushed a hand forward. "Jonas Russable," the man said. "I'm in mining supplies. With Hancock and Morrison, Cincinnati. You?"

"Custis Long," Longarm introduced himself. He did not particularly want to lie to the open-faced and friendly drummer, so he neglected to state any occupation to the man.

Of course, Longarm realized, as far as he knew this smiling Russable fellow might actually be the leader of the White Hoods. Still, that seemed unlikely.

"Smoke?" Russable offered him a cheap rum crook. Longarm would rather have smoked a used handkerchief.

"No, thanks. I have my own." Longarm nipped off the tip of one of his cheroots and accepted a light off Russable's already half-smoked crook. "Thanks."

"I haven't seen you in Thunderbird Canyon before, Mr. Long," Russable said, obviously hinting for further information.

"First trip," Longarm admitted.

"You, uh, are in mining supplies too, I take it?"

"What? Oh." Longarm smiled. The fellow was worried about competition, he guessed. Afraid his meal ticket might be cancelled or at least reduced if someone else came in to contest his prices. "No. I'm looking around for, uh, speculations. So to speak."

Russable's smile became broader. "Ah. Very good, Mr. Long." He had nothing to fear from Longarm.

"You know the area, I take it?" Longarm asked, making small talk.

"Oh, yes. Twice a month, I come up here. Regular as a clock."

"That's interesting." It wasn't. There was little Longarm could think of that would be more boring than having to do something—anything—with the regularity of clockwork.

38

"Used to frighten me, I must say," Russable said.

"Really? I hadn't realized Thunderbird Canyon was that rough a camp."

Russable laughed like Longarm had just cracked a particularly funny joke.

Longarm raised an eyebrow.

Still laughing, Russable explained, "The camp is entirely pleasant, I assure you. After all, where is anyone to run to if there should be trouble? It's a small town, really, and everyone knows everyone else. No, sir, you need fear no danger in Thunderbird Canyon. It's this damnable train ride that used to frighten me so."

"Really?" Longarm looked around. Russable must be an easily frightened man if this bothered him. The narrow-gauge train was crawling along a ledge a dozen feet or so above a roaring cascade of a mountain white-water stream, but there was hardly anything frightening about that. Not that Longarm could see. The roadbed was wide enough, if barely, the rock was solid, and the foamy water of the river was a safe distance below. Perhaps in springtime during the snow-melt season there might be reason for concern, but certainly not now.

Russable chuckled but did not elaborate. The two men leaned on the railing that surrounded the platform and smoked their cigars in a silence that was companionable rather than strained.

The grade increased slightly, and the tiny locomotive slowed to the strain of the pull, even though the long string of ore cars ahead were running empty. Russable chuckled again for some inexplicable reason. He had finished his vile-smelling rum crook, but remained where he was at the rail.

"Don't feel like having your eardrums shattered today?" Longarm asked.

Russable grinned. "Something like that."

The leaping water of the mountain stream fell farther and farther below them as the railbed mounted the side of the steep-walled canyon. Now there was probably more than a hundred feet of drop to the roaring water.

The train slowed again with a clank and a groan, and Longarm was glad he had a hold on the railing, or he might have lost his balance. The grade was quite sharp now, and the mountain river below was looking farther and farther away until it appeared quite small.

Russable's grin turned sly.

There was more shaking and shuddering along the string of cars, and Russable chuckled.

"What the hell?"

Russable hooked a thumb forward. "Take a look," he suggested.

Longarm moved to the side of the platform and leaned out to see ahead of the passenger coach.

There was absolutely nothing there save blue sky and the towering rock wall on the opposite side of the narrow gorge of Thunderbird Canyon.

Nothing.

Then Longarm spotted a golden eagle soaring on the gusty wind currents of the canyon air. *A good fifty feet beneath the chuffing train*. Longarm smiled. So that was it. Russable was afraid of heights. Hell, they didn't bother Longarm. He had more serious things to concern himself with.

The cars ahead of the passenger coach had already disappeared around a bend in the narrow track. Now the passenger coach too swung round the curve with a lurch.

The damned drummer was laughing again.

"Now look down," Russable suggested.

Longarm shrugged. If it made the fool happy.

The river appeared quite small now. They were a good two hundred fifty, three hundred feet above it and still climbing. But except for that . . .

"Off the back of the platform," Russable said.

Longarm shrugged again and returned to the rear of the platform.

There was nothing under his feet but distance and white

water. Somewhere down there, beneath rails and ties that seemed suspended in thin air, he could see a runty juniper clinging to a crack in the stark, barren rock.

In spite of himself, Longarm felt his stomach lurch, and he grabbed tight to the railing until his knuckles whitened.

"Like I said," Russable said calmly, "used to scare the shit out of me." He was still grinning.

"Jesus," Longarm whispered.

Now that the train was well onto this stretch and there was some track behind that he could examine, Longarm saw that the original mule trail would have been barely wide enough for a pack animal to negotiate. No wonder Morey Fahnwell had said it used to be a hell of a trip where some mules were lost now and then. One misstep off that ledge, and it was a straight shot down for a hell of a distance.

In order to build the rail bed here the engineers—Longarm damn sure would not have wanted to work on *that* piece of road—had had to cantilever half the damn road out over the edge with stout steel braces set into the rock.

The entire outer half of the train was running over empty space, held up by steel supports and wooden ties.

"Oh, shit," Longarm muttered.

"Yeah," Russable agreed happily. "I never thought I was scared of heights neither, until I started to come up here." He reached inside his coat and pulled out first a pair of the nasty rum crooks, then a silver flask. "Join me?"

Longarm accepted the drink *and* the smoke with thanks.

"It isn't far like this," Russable told him. "A quarter mile or so. We'll be back over solid ledge in another minute or two."

Longarm didn't answer, but he did take another welcome, warming swallow of the salesman's liquor.

"Shee-it!" he said.

Russable chuckled and recapped his flask.

The train jolted and shook at an unusually abrupt junction of the rails.

"There. Now you can look down again without risking your linen."

Longarm looked. Under his feet this time there was once again the comforting presence of rock and cinders and ties buried solidly in crushed ballast.

"Whew!"

"Yeah," Russable agreed.

"If I'd known that was coming I think I'd've stayed inside and played with the brats."

"It isn't so bad from here in," Russable told him. "I guess I should've warned you, but . . ." He laughed.

Longarm shook his head and smiled. "If I knew you better, Mr. Russable, I might punch you in the mouth. Instead, how about I treat for a drink after we get to town? Hell, maybe I'll get to know you well enough that I *can* punch you in the mouth."

Russable threw his head back and roared. "You're on, Mr. Long. Say, the hotel bar a seven?"

Longarm grinned at the man. "I'll see you there."

Chapter 9

Thunderbird Canyon was a typical mining camp, not a particularly large or prosperous one, set along the sides of the canyon that gave it its name, and extending in a narrow strip on both sides of the stream that had carved the gorge through so much solid rock.

There was so little room at the bottom of the canyon that virtually none of the ground there was level. Even the twin streets that flanked the small, churning river canted at a slight angle, and every house or building in the camp had to be built with its back to the rock and the front end supported by pilings and reached by steep stairs.

It was the sort of place where if a man walked in his sleep he would likely tumble out of his own window and fall onto the next fellow's roof.

There was not room enough for a railroad turntable, and no room either for much in the way of shunt rails. Apparently the train remained pretty much made up the way it was, and the little locomotive had to back the whole way down to Meade Park on the morning down-runs.

There were two sets of mine buildings—crushers and separators and whatever else—starting high on the east wall of the canyon and dribbling down the mountainside, along with the tailings dumps of pale waste rock from the shafts that extended somewhere inside the mountain. To the west there was another mine, making three in all.

The two on the eastward mountain were able to use simple gravity to transfer their ore into hoppers to feed the rail cars, while ore from the western-side mine had to be hauled across a bridge and loaded onto the cars with much more labor.

Between the mines and the buildings below were several sets of huge, barnlike buildings that probably were the company boarding houses for the underground miners.

Down below, close to the river, were the saloons, restaurants, whorehouses, stores, public buildings... everything else that was needed or that would turn a profit for someone.

Longarm did not have to fret himself with choosing a hotel. There was only one. It simplified things.

He carried his things across the muddy planks of the bridge and checked into the hotel, Jonas Russable ahead of him.

"Room seven," the clerk said. "Second floor rear."

"I'll have it to myself, I hope," Longarm asked.

The desk clerk gave him a look that was close to being pitying. "Glory, mister, if there ain't anybody else already, there damn sure ain't gonna be anybody later. Couldn't be till tomorra's train run."

"I keep forgetting," Longarm said.

Surely the camp couldn't be *that* isolated.

"Nobody to share with tonight," the clerk assured him. "If you want a promise o' privacy tomorra night it'll cost you extra. But I won't charge you that till tomorra, and you don't hafta tell me what you decide till the train's due tomorra afternoon."

"That sounds fair." Longarm collected his key and paid for the room in cash. A voucher would have been more convenient, but that would have tipped the clerk and anyone the man chose to tell that there was a federal deputy in town.

When he signed the register, Longarm scanned the book for the names of other recent arrivals, even flipping it back a page. None of the names were familiar. And there were not all that many, anyway. If the White Hoods were already in place in Thunderbird Canyon, they were either one damned small gang these days or they had a local contact they could stay with.

"Looking for somebody in particular?" the clerk asked.

"No. Just a habit. You know how it is when you're on the road. Always looking for a friendly face. That's all."

"Yeah, if you say so." Longarm gathered that the hotel clerk was not much of a traveling man himself.

"Up the stairs an' to your right," the man said.

"Thanks."

The room was nothing much, but it was reasonably clean and the sheets were fresh. Longarm had stayed in worse.

The lock on the door was a flimsy thing that damned near could be picked with a thumbnail, and there was no bolt on the inside. Longarm put his bag and Winchester in a tall wardrobe and placed a few telltales after he closed the doors. Not that he expected trouble here, no one in town knowing who or what he was, but a little caution never hurt.

The telltales, of course, would not stop anyone from robbing him if they wanted to, but at least he would know if anybody was interested in his baggage but did not want him to find out about it.

It was late afternoon, and he debated between rest after last night's ride and eating. Sleep won out. He could eat later when he went down to meet Russable in the bar. He kicked off his boots and stretched out on top of the bedspread.

Normal procedure called for a courtesy visit to the local sheriff or town marshal, whichever turned out to be appropriate here, but that could wait too. Right now he needed to get some of the pounding out of the back of his head and some of the grittiness out of his eyes. His ass was dragging, and that was the simple truth of it.

Chapter 10

Feeling considerably refreshed after an hour of sleep, Longarm washed the last cobwebs out of his brain with cold water from the pitcher left in his room, and went down to the bar.

Russable was already there and several drinks ahead of him. Longarm ordered a bottle of rye whiskey and a huge steak—some of Morey Fahnwell's beef, no doubt—and was feeling practically human by the time he had a couple drinks in him and the meal to keep them company.

The salesman leaned forward and winked when Longarm pushed his plate away. "Now I think you should come with me, and I'll show you some of the sights of Thunderbird Canyon," he suggested.

"Hell, Jonas, I didn't think this camp would have any sights worth seeing."

"Just one. But it's a humdinger. Matter of fact, this particular sight is the reason I always make my weekend layover here. I make the circuit every two weeks, you know, and every time I'm on the road I make it a point to stop here for the whole weekend."

"Now what kind of sight would it be that a man'd want to see every other week?"

Russable snorted. "This little ol' mining camp, Custis, has the finest, classiest, best quality house of ill repute between Kansas City and San Francisco."

"You sound like a man who's tested them all to decide on that, too."

Russable grinned at him and winked again. "I won't say I've hit them all, Custis, but I've done my best."

Longarm had to force a smile in response. Two minutes earlier the salesman had been bragging about what a fine and understanding wife he had. Of course, it was Russable's business what he wanted to do. But Longarm's opinion was that it was not very damned respectful of his own wife for the man to tell both tales to a total stranger in practically the same breath.

"Best liquor and hottest damn tamales in the business, Custis," Russable went on, unaware of Longarm's shift of opinion about him. "Mexican whores, most of them, shipped up from someplace down south. And can they wiggle? Let me tell you." He leaned closer and poked Longarm in the ribs, which was not one of the tall deputy's favorite gestures anyway. "Hot as these girls are, I'd swear they must stuff chili peppers up their pussies between customers."

"It sounds interesting," Longarm lied, "but there are some folks I need to see. Check a few things out. You know." He had given the salesman only a vague cover story as his reason for being in Thunderbird Canyon, so there was no reason for him to elaborate. If Longarm just left it alone now, Russable would be able to come up with a reasonable business explanation without Longarm's help.

"That's a shame, Custis. Kinda adds to the fun to have a friend along, if you know what I mean. Pick girls and then swap back an' forth for the seconds. See who can get which one to holler the loudest. Like that." The man snickered.

Longarm looked away before he rolled his eyes. The man's gullibility was incredible. A whore, any whore, will moan and squeal the loudest for whoever pays the most. Hell, anybody dry behind the ears ought to understand that.

"Yeah, well, I'm sorry, but I expect I've got to pass, Jonas."

"Whatever you say, Custis. Maybe tomorrow night."

"Sure. Maybe tomorrow night." By tomorrow night

Longarm expected to be busy guarding an unspecified number of White Hood Gang members, of course. But if the innocent lie would get this drummer off his back, it was worthwhile.

Russable collected his hat and left, neglecting to pay for the drinks he had had before Longarm joined him. The amount for them was added to Longarm's bill, which did not please him a whole hell of a lot.

Longarm gave the salesman time to get wherever he was going, then paid the tab and walked out onto the narrow, sloping street.

The mountain air was crisp and chilly, and the sun had long since disappeared somewhere off toward Oregon. Thunderbird Canyon was ablaze with lights, though, including the mines high on the slopes to either side. Apparently the silver veins they were following were rich enough to justify having shifts work around the clock.

Longarm got directions from one of the many miners crowding the streets and walked down to the sheriff's office.

The sheriff's office was housed on the top floor of a building that also served as the county courthouse and city hall. It was an unusual combination, but probably no one wanted to waste too much space and energy on the construction of separate county and municipal facilities. In a camp like this one, whatever was built today could well be abandoned tomorrow. As soon as the ore played out the whole shooting match would pull stakes and go away. This time next year Thunderbird Canyon could be a ghost town. Ten years and it would be hard to find the foundations where buildings once had stood.

An unshaven deputy sheriff whose red-rimmed eyes and scarlet-veined nose gave him an undesirable character reference was busy putting another drunk into a cell when Longarm entered the small, unkempt office at the top of the stairs.

"Be with you in a minute, mister." The deputy unlocked the prisoner's cuffs and ducked as the drunk threw a slow, sloppy, looping punch toward him. The deputy thumped the drunk on the back of the head and shoved him sprawling onto the cell floor. The man landed facedown and began to groan softly. The deputy ignored the drunk's problems and closed and locked the cell door on him.

"Now," he said, blinking as if trying to recall if he recognized the tall visitor. "What c'n I do you for?" He cackled at his own originality.

"I wanted to have a word with the sheriff," Longarm said politely.

"The sherf's busy. You c'n talk to me. I'm his chief deppity." The man tossed the cell keys onto a desk that occupied most of the floor space in the place, slouched into the chair behind it, and propped his boots up on its surface.

Chief deputy? Longarm thought. The chief deputy here appeared to be a man Billy Vail would hesitate to hire to sweep out the cells, much less to fill them.

"My business is with the sheriff himself," Longarm explained gently. "Where might I find him?"

The chief deputy's face twisted into a scowl, and he dropped his boots to the floor with a loud thump and sat upright so he could glare at Longarm better. "Don't you be getting smartass with me, you son of a bitch, or I'll—"

The man's eyes went wide, and there was a sudden pallor underneath the unshaven beard stubble on his cheeks. All of a sudden he was no longer sitting at the sheriff's desk.

Almost before he had time to register that the visitor was moving, the chief deputy was being hauled upright by a strong hand clenched into the front of his shirt, and he was hanging suspended from the visitor's fist. They were nose to nose. The visitor did not look so mild and polite anymore.

"Smartass?" Longarm asked in a voice that remained deceptively calm and even. "It's smartass for somebody to ask to see the sheriff? No, Chief Deputy, I'll tell you what's smartass. Smartass is the way I'm going to take that badge off your vest and plant it four fingers deep inside your left nostril if you give me any shit. Smartass is what I get when I'm tired and I've got work to do and there's some asshole wanting to play the bigshot with me. And smart is what your ass is going to do when I get done kicking it. Just for the hell of it. Now I ask you again, friend, where might I find the sheriff of this county?"

Throughout, Longarm's voice was controlled and soft, never rising a decibel, even when he lifted the chief deputy, shook him vigorously, and deposited him back into his chair.

The chief deputy cringed like a whipped dog and licked at suddenly dry lips. "I . . . you c'n find the sherf at Jessie's place. Most likely."

"Thank you," Longarm said coldly. "You've been very helpful."

"Yeah, uh . . ."

"You'd best shut up now," Longarm suggested, "or I might take a notion to get mad."

"No need f'r that, mister," the chief deputy said hastily.

"Jessie's place?"

"Yes, sir."

"Thank you for the assistance, Chief Deputy."

Longarm left, hoping the chief deputy would not vent his frustrated impotence on the hapless drunk who was still groaning on the cell floor.

Chapter 11

Jessie's place turned out to be Jessie's Place, as Longarm discovered even before he climbed the long stairway to the front door.

The place announced its purpose with a pair of red-glassed coach lamps flanking the ornate door, and by the heavily shuttered and draped windows on all three stories of the tall, narrow structure. Lamplight glimmered dimly from behind each of the covered windows. Jessie's Place apparently did a very good trade.

His knock was answered by an attractive woman in an evening gown. The hostess, possibly the madam herself, was tall, her carriage a study in practiced elegance. Longarm guessed she was in her forties, but damned well preserved and still prettier than nearly any "working girl" a man could expect to find in such an out-of-the-way place. She wore—and needed—very little makeup, just enough to emphasize her natural attributes. That in itself was most unusual in a whorehouse.

Longarm removed his Stetson to her, and she gave him a warm and seemingly genuine smile.

"My," she said, "the gentleman is not only handsome, he is gallant. I believe I am in love, sir." She laughed brightly and stepped back so he could enter.

"Thank you, ma'am."

"My name is Jessie," she said. "What may I call you?" He noticed that she did not ask his name, only what she could call him. The lady was discreet as well as pretty.

"I'm Custis Long, Jessie. I came here to see one of your, uh, patrons. But now I believe I have other reasons to be pleased I met you."

Jessie rolled her eyes. "Oh my, Mr. Long. Keep this up and I shall be tempted to return to, shall we say, an *active* pursuit of the business." Her bantering tone said that she didn't mean it, but the compliment was there and he appreciated it for what it was.

On an impulse Longarm made a leg and bowed over her gloved hand. "The unfortunate thing, Miss Jessie, is that now I couldn't possibly be satisfied with the company of anyone but the lady of the house."

She laughed, obviously pleased.

"Would you care for a drink, Mr. Long?"

"If you will have one with me."

She led him into a parlor that was decorated in the overplush, overstuffed, red-velvet style that was for some reason common to first-class whorehouses and seated him on a scarlet settee.

There were several other men in the place and a few of the working girls. The men were dressed several cuts above the norm for working men. Undoubtedly Jessie's Place catered to foremen and above, no riffraff allowed.

The girls Longarm could see in the parlor were dark-eyes, raven-haired beauties. They were all young, all nicely dressed, and all exceptionally pretty. Of Mexican extraction each of them, so this would be the place that brought Jonas Russable to Thunderbird Canyon for his weekend layovers. No wonder the salesman was so high on it. Miss Jessie's girls were fine-looking ladies. Every one of them looked fresh and lovely and clean enough to eat. Or be eaten by, whichever appealed.

Jessie sat at Longarm's side, one arm draped over the cozily encircling arm of the settee. She lifted a finger in a seemingly casual gesture and within seconds there was a young and heartbreakingly pretty Mexican girl standing attentively in front of her. Appearances aside, Longarm realized, Miss Jessie ran a tight ship indeed.

"The gentleman would like a drink, Rosalie."

"Yes'm." Rosalie dropped her eyes and ducked into a brief, submissive curtsy.

"Rye whiskey, please."

Rosalie nodded without looking at him. "And you, ma'am?" Her voice was heavily accented but certainly understandable enough. The girl looked and sounded no more than sixteen, if that. Her breasts, half-visible over the low-cut bodice of her gown, were taut and small and flawless. Longarm felt an unbidden stirring of interest even though his thoughts were on other matters right now.

"Yes," Jessie said. "A small glass." Her preference did not have to be stated. When Rosalie brought the tiny, tulip-shaped glass to her on a silver tray, along with Longarm's general measure of fine rye, he saw that it was a ruby-colored wine of some sort.

Rosalie served the drinks, curtsied again, and returned to her duties beside a florid-faced, half-drunk gentleman wearing a stickpin that would have cost enough to support a large family for a year or better.

"To your very good health, Mr. Long."

"And to yours, Jessie."

He tasted the rye. It was as good as he expected it to be.

"Now to business, Mr. Long. Can I not tempt you with one of my young ladies? Fifty dollars. And there are absolutely no . . . restrictions . . . as to what you might wish to do with them." Her smile this time was tight and cold.

Longarm blinked. Fifty dollars! The price was staggering. It was more than most family men could earn in a month.

Jessie noticed his reaction, and her smile became broader if no warmer. "No restrictions at all, Mr. Long. These luscious little doves from down south are, shall we say, easily replaceable whenever necessary. And I *do* want my gentlemen friends to enjoy themselves." Her smile was professional and greedy, even cruel.

Longarm felt a chill invade his belly and drive away the warmth of the rye. The swell of interest he had felt when looking at pretty, vulnerable, young Rosalie was gone as quickly and as completely as if it had never been.

"Are you telling me . . . ?"

"This is a *very* special house, Mr. Long. I am telling you that we shall be pleased to accommodate any taste, however exceptional."

There was that smile again. But now Longarm found the expression chilling rather than welcome. All of a sudden Jessie reminded him of a cat. A big cat. A mountain lion with all its merciless and deadly beauty. Jesus!

"Maybe later," he said, struggling to keep a stammer out of his voice. He felt unnerved. Pissed off, really. He looked at the girls who were in the room, and now they looked not so much pretty to him as pathetic. Anything a man wanted? Custis Long knew from long and sometimes bitter experience with the human race that "anything" could cover a whole lot of very ugly territory. And Jessie had not been exaggerating when she said "anything." She had also said the girls were easily replaced. Jesus!

"You did mention a desire to meet someone here," Jessie conceded. "Naturally we mustn't interrupt any of our gentlemen. Are you sure you wouldn't like to enjoy yourself while you wait?"

"No, I . . ." The refusal came automatically to his lips. Then he thought better of it and forced himself to give the madam a smile that he did not mean in the slightest. "Come to think of it, Jessie, there's really no reason why I shouldn't have a little fun while I wait. You did say the girls will accommodate any desire, right?"

"Absolutely, Mr. Long. Anything whatsoever."

His smile was genuine this time. "Then I would enjoy some time with Rosalie there."

"An excellent choice, Mr. Long. Dear Rosalie is quite new to us. She has barely completed her training here. I am sure she will satisfy."

"I'm sure she will," Longarm said with a pleased anticipation that he did not have to fake. "And if the sheriff should return to the parlor while I'm occupied, would you delay him here for me, please?"

"My pleasure, Mr. Long." She continued to sit and smile at him as if she were waiting for something. It took him a moment to realize what it was. Then he remembered.

Fifty dollars in cash was what the no-longer-attractive whore wanted. The expense would damn near clean him out of cash. But it was going to be worth it.

And after all, tomorrow was when the White Hoods were supposed to strike. After the arrival of the afternoon train he wouldn't have to worry any longer about keeping his occupation a secret. Then he could pay for whatever he needed with vouchers.

He reached deep into his pocket and gave the bitch her money.

"Thank you, Mr. Long." Jessie lifted her finger once again, and slim, pretty little Rosalie appeared soundlessly in front of them. Now that he knew what was up in this house of horrors, Longarm could see the pain of frightened anticipation in the girl's downcast eyes.

"You may escort the gentleman to room five, Rosalie."

"Yes, ma'am."

Without ever once looking Longarm in the face the girl took his hand with a light, trembling touch and led him toward the stairs.

Chapter 12

The room was small and surprisingly plain after the luxury exhibited downstairs. There was a reason for that, though, a reason that was evident in the peculiar furnishings of the place. In addition to a sturdy bed and hard mattress with no covers except a single sheet, there were the odd trappings of a "special" whorehouse.

A wall rack that held a selection of quirts and whips and willow switches. A box of leather and steel fetters. Ropes and gags and hatpins and even, incredibly, a razor and strop for those whose quirks demanded blood and serious pain.

Longarm looked at all of it in partial disbelief. He had been expecting it in a way. But now, confronted with the reality of it, his mind stubbornly refused to accept it until the second or third inspection of the vile chamber.

He looked at Rosalie and realized only then that while he had been staring at the embellishments of a virtual torture chamber, the young Mexican girl had been calmly removing her gown. Now she dropped the garment onto an oddly-shaped stool that had manacles and steel anklets attached to its legs. Naked—and admittedly lovely, but with her eyes still downcast and unable to meet his—she turned to face him.

She stood with her chin low, arms slack, and shoulders slumped. Longarm could not begin to guess what she expected him to do to her—not with her but *to* her now—but whatever it was she offered no resistance. She stood mute and accepting before him.

She was a lovely girl, although her body was flawed. Flawed not by nature, but by plan. Her nipples were scabbed and misshapen from something that had been recently done, and there were the welts and bruises of a beating on her hips.

Longarm cleared his throat, the sound loud and awkward in the silence of the small room. "I, uh, have a special request for you."

She nodded without looking at him.

"First thing, Rosalie, I'd like you to turn around, please."

She turned, posing naked for his inspection, as if that were the most normal and natural thing for anyone to possibly do.

Longarm felt a kernel of ice develop deep in his belly. The teenage girl's back was a latticework of fading welts and cuts. Someone had whipped her severely within the past few weeks. What had Whoremistress Jessie said? Rosalie had undergone a "training" period. These marks on her slender body must have resulted from part of that training. And surely no one, not even the most desperate and hungry whore, would willingly allow any person to cause her such pain. Not for any amount of money.

"I, uh, I was told I can do anything in this room, Rosalie. Is that right?"

"Yes, sir. I will do as you say. Anyt'ing." She was still facing away from him, but he could hear the hopelessness in her voice. The tone was what he might have imagined should come from a grave. And he could see the slight trembling in her shoulders and across her marred back.

"Anything at all, right?"

"I do what you want."

"And if for some reason you don't?"

"I do what you want. Anyt'ing, sir."

"You might not like what I want you to do, Rosalie. You might think it's kinda strange."

"Anyt'ing you want, I do it for you," she said softly. There was a small catch of fear in her voice, but there was no hesitation whatsoever.

"Good," Longarm said with a smile. "The first thing I want you to do, Rosalie, is to put your dress back on."

Unquestioning, the girl bent to retrieve her gown and dressed again. Still she faced away from him. He had not yet told her to turn again after once instructing her to face away. Obviously this girl, barely more than a child, had been trained to total obedience.

Perhaps, he thought, this would be easier for both of them if she stayed facing in that direction.

"Now sit on the edge of the bed, Rosalie, facing toward the wall over there."

She did as she was told.

Longarm wiped a suddenly sweaty palm on his corduroy trousers and helped himself to an uncomfortable seat on the strangely shaped stool.

"Now the thing that really pleases me, Rosalie, and what I want you to do for me, is to tell me about yourself. Everything about yourself. Particularly how you came to be here at Jessie's Place and what you had to learn before you started working here. And it all has to be the truth, Rosalie, or it won't please me. Do you understand what I want from you?"

She shrugged.

Hell, he realized, she understood nothing about what *any* of Jessie's customers would want from her.

But if that was what the customer wanted, that was what the customer would get.

She had been taught to give obedience that was instant and complete. However abnormal, Longarm's request was just another thing she had to do. So without hesitation, little Rosalie began to do as she was taught and please her customer.

Chapter 13

Longarm was feeling pretty chipper when he came down the stairs forty-five minutes later. He was relaxed and ready for tomorrow's business. Better yet, a gray-haired, distinguished-looking man with a badge pinned to his vest was lounging on the settee with Jessie.

"Mr. Long," Jessie said graciously, extending a manicured hand to him. "Do you already know our sheriff?" There was no mention of Rosalie, no questions about whether the girl needed any sort of help upstairs. The whore treated the whole business like nothing might have happened at all. She was a cool bitch, Longarm thought, and no longer attractive to him in the slightest.

"No, I don't," he said.

"Mr. Long, Sheriff Paul Markham. Sheriff, Mr. Long." Smiling, she rose to her feet in a fluid motion. "Now, if you gentlemen would excuse me . . ." She left them, joining another customer on the far side of the room.

"Jessie said there was someone who wanted to see me," Markham said. Longarm could smell liquor heavy on the man's breath, though he did not give any appearance of being under the influence.

"That's right, Sheriff, but what I have to discuss with you has to be confidential."

"My dear sir, anything and everything that happens inside these walls is completely confidential. That is only one of the many attractions of the place." He winked, and for a moment Longarm thought he was about to get a nudge in the ribs. Instead, the sheriff motioned for one of the girls to come. "A drink while we talk, Mr. Long?"

Longarm gestured impatiently for the girl to go away. He leaned close to the sheriff and in a voice too low to carry said, "We are going to go down to your office to do our talking, Markham. And we are going to do it now, sir." There was no threat in his voice, not exactly, but there was considerable steel there.

"Yes, uh, perhaps we could do that, Mr. Long," the sheriff said. He stood and airily tossed toward Jessie, "The gentleman and I have business, dear. I shall be back shortly. You'll make the arrangements?"

Jessie smiled brightly, like she had never heard anything nicer in her entire, sheltered life. "Of course, Paul. Everything will be quite ready for you."

Longarm said nothing, but Paul Markham would have no free time this night for whatever weird pleasures were customarily "arranged" for him in this house of ugliness.

The two men went outside into the night.

It was a funny thing, but the mountain air that a little while ago had seemed so clean and invigorating now felt only cold and faintly depressing to Long.

There was no sign of the chief deputy in the quiet office when Longarm and Markham got there. The drunk had managed to crawl onto the bare, wooden slats of one of the cots in his cell and was sleeping off his excesses. His nose was somewhat out of position, and the lower part of his face was a mask of dried blood from where he had hit the floor when the deputy jugged him, but he seemed relatively unharmed.

Markham took his seat behind the desk and knitted his fingers together on the front of his vest. No propping of feet for him.

He was a fine-looking figure of a man, Longarm realized. Distinguished, even dignified looking. He looked every inch a bright and capable wielder of law and authority.

"Now, sir, what is so urgent that you must take me away from my evening relaxations?"

Relaxations. Was *that* what it was called in Idaho? Where Longarm came from there were other names for it. But no matter. Right now there were other fish to fry.

Longarm searched his coat pockets to find first his badge and then the duplicate copy of the telegram from Fort Smith, Arkansas, that had started this whole thing. He showed both to Markham.

"Ah. Oh, yes. Mmmm." Markham examined both the badge and the telegraph form with care, then returned them to their owner. "Now I understand."

"Do you?"

"Of course. Naturally I do, Marshal. And naturally I will be glad to cooperate with you in every way possible."

Markham smiled, and Longarm felt relief flood through him. After meeting the sheriff's choice for a chief deputy —and, honestly, knowing something now about the place where the elected sheriff here chose to spend his free time —Longarm had been getting damn well worried about the likelihood of success here against the White Hoods. Markham, though, seemed entirely willing to help. The first hurdle had been cleared.

"Thanks, Sheriff." Longarm crossed his legs and pulled out a cheroot.

It wasn't midnight yet, and the two of them had fourteen, fifteen hours to work out the details of how this one was going to go. And when they were done, by damn, the White Hoods would be broken and on their way to well-deserved prison terms.

Yes, by damn, Longarm thought, things were coming along very nicely for a change.

Chapter 14

Henry removed his spectacles, took a freshly washed but unironed handkerchief from his hip pocket, and carefully cleaned and polished the lenses of the glasses. It was something to do. Something better than screaming and throwing things, which was what he truly wanted to do right now.

He turned toward the conductor, who was sipping hot coffee and thumbing through the pages of a dog-eared *Police Gazette*. "Can't you—"

"Sorry, gov'nor. Not till the order comes through." He pointed needlessly toward the signal box, which still showed the damnable red flipper for the damnable train waiting endlessly on the damnable siding. The freight— Henry had "saved" all of an hour and three quarters by taking the westbound freight out of Cheyenne instead of waiting for the through passenger—had been sitting on the siding for five hours now, waiting for God knew what. The westbound passenger had swept by them several hours before, and still the freight sat immobile on the siding, and no amount of persuasion or threatening or cursing could convince the crew to violate their orders and get the freight moving west again.

"But—"

"Sorry, gov'nor. We don't move until we get our green signal. You know that."

Henry chafed and champed, but he knew it would do no good whatsoever.

"That signal could be broken," he said at one point.

"If it is," the conductor said patiently, "there'll be a repair crew along by an' by." He turned another page and leaned down to inspect more closely an advertisement that promised a cure for baldness. "I wonder if this really works. They have testamonials. See? Surely they couldn't lie about a thing like that. Not in print, surely. I wond—"

"Can't you send someone at least to look at the box? See if the thing is working properly? Or you could wire ahead to Rock Springs to verify the stop order. Can't you do at least that much?"

The conductor gave him a dirty look and went back to his perusal of the advertisement.

Henry turned to face the flimsy wall of the caboose, doubled up a fist, and hammered the wall hard enough to make the thin slats vibrate along the full length of the sooty crew car.

"That won't do you any good, Marshal," a brakeman said patiently. "We're stuck here until they tell us different."

The knowledge did not make Henry feel better in the slightest. Groaning aloud, he spun about and began once again to pace back and forth along the length of the narrow aisle of his damnable prison.

Chapter 15

Longarm pinched the bridge of his nose and rubbed at his eyes, but the relief was more imagined than real. His head was throbbing, and he felt like his skull might burst at any moment. Another drink of Markham's horrible bourbon might help, although that too would be an illusion of comfort and not the real thing. What he really needed was twelve hours of sleep.

The ride from Snake Creek to Meade Park trying to beat the departure of the Thunderbird Run...the trip up here and a blessed few hours of sleep...now he and the distinguished-looking but unbelievably stupid sheriff had been up all the damned night again arguing over details of how they were supposed to trap and capture one of the slickest damn robbery gangs to come down the pike since Bert the Poet.

Jesus!

Markham's entire force consisted of himself, Chief Deputy Roland Mayes—who Longarm wouldn't trust to wipe his own ass correctly—and a Deputy Charlie Frye, who looked to be fifteen, and a damned innocent fifteen at that. The kid was a skinny little bit of a thing with biceps like twigs and no armament more serious than a whittling knife. Longarm suspected that no one in town would trust the boy with an actual firearm. And Longarm couldn't blame them. If he was given a revolver to carry he likely wouldn't be strong enough to lift and aim the thing.

"Look," Longarm said again, repeating territory often

covered through the predawn hours, "there is no way this local force of yours is going to have enough firepower to make the White Hoods do any more than laugh when you jump out to face them. We *have* to get some help from the mine security people. We just have to, that's all."

"Now, damnit, Marshal Long," the sheriff had not been invited to address Longarm by nickname, "you told me yourself, right up front, that this has to be a job with inside connections. Otherwise, why try and take the train here. It has to be an inside operation, and there has to be some plan for the getaway that we haven't discovered yet. Although, of course, we shall as soon as we have some of those gents in our cells. Then, sir, we shall get the truth out of them."

"And I am telling you, Sheriff, that four guns—"

"Three," Markham interrupted. "My forte is administration, actually. But three men properly placed and properly armed can cow any group of sneak thieves. I am convinced of this."

Markham seemed quite unperturbed by the thought of sending Longarm and two useless yokels after the whole damned White Hood outfit when that train arrived in just a few hours.

What did disturb him, Longarm was convinced, was the idea of sharing the glory with any private force of mine security guards. The man would rather risk losing the White Hoods than share the political benefit of the capture. There was no point in asking it outright, of course, but Longarm would be willing to bet his next year's pay that someone heading one of the mine security forces was hoping to challenge Paul Markham come the next elections.

Longarm still couldn't decide, though, if the dumb bastard really believed his pitiful pair of deputies could help. Maybe he thought Longarm was going to be able to bring in the whole bunch on his own. Then again, maybe the idiot would rather put on an unsuccessful fireworks show for the benefit of the voters, and lose the White Hoods, than give his election opponent the leverage of participating in the capture.

Whatever the truth of the matter—and Longarm would probably never know where that truth lay—Markham was resisting him at every suggestion.

The chief deputy was not helping either. Mayes spent most of his time glaring at Longarm in sullen silence. The rest of the time he was looking for excuses to step out into the hall or over to the cells so he could take a nip from the pint bottle he was carrying. Longarm could not believe the man thought he was fooling anyone about the bottle. The thing was crammed into a pocket that was too small, and the weight of it pulled his coat down half off his shoulder.

Come to think of it, Longarm realized, maybe Mayes *was* fooling Markham and young Frye. If they did see it, they certainly were able to successfully pretend otherwise.

By the time the train arrived from Meade Park, Longarm fully expected Roland Mayes to be passed out drunk whatever they decided to do by then.

Longarm rubbed aching eyes and tried again. "The White Hoods are a gang of ten, twelve men, Sheriff. They know what they're doing. They hit hard, they hit fast, and no man who's ever seen one of their faces has every survived the experience. They aren't afraid to kill people for their own protection. They are *good,* I'm telling you, and they could make hash of any force of just three or four men. Even three or four of our federal deputies." That part was just so much bullshit, of course. If Smiley and Dutch were here to back him, or Billy Vail and Henry even, Longarm would have no doubt at all about the White Hoods heading for the cells. But there was no point to telling Sheriff Paul Markham that. Smiley and Dutch and Henry and the marshal were *not* here, and that was the end of that.

"And I am telling you, sir, that my force of deputies can handle this matter. Which, I hasten to mention, is within my jurisdiction. I am in charge of this operation, Marshal Long. Any interference by you, sir, and I shall make an immediate protest to your superiors in Denver and in Washington, and . . ."

Yeah, yeah, yeah. Longarm had heard all that before, more times than he could count or wanted to. The man was farting through his teeth. Longarm's attention wandered while Markham continued to spout off.

The only reason Longarm hadn't put all three of them and a bottle to keep them all company into one of their own jails and gone off to make his own arrangements with the mine security people was that that asshole Mayes had already as good as said he would fuck up the whole deal with a lot of public armwaving if Markham didn't get his ignorant way. Even though the case was under federal jurisdiction.

If Markham didn't get to set the rules, nobody was going to be allowed to play the game. Talk about taking your toys and going home. . . .

And that was one thing about the damn White Hoods. They were good, all right. And wary. The least hint of anything being out of place in their plans, and they would fade off into the distance so slick nobody would ever know for sure if they'd been there or not.

Once before, Longarm remembered, a particularly efficient sheriff down in New Mexico got a tip on them, passed along by a disgruntled whore who overheard some talk. The White Hoods were supposed to be hitting a bank just before dawn one moonless night. The local sheriff had pulled in all his deputies and set up an ambush hours ahead of time.

Turned out the badge-carrying ambushers sat on their butts until the bank opened for business the next day, and then everybody went off to have breakfast and catch up on missed sleep. There was never a peep out of the robbers.

Later that day the sheriff heard from a man with a weak bladder that when he had gotten up in the night he had heard a dozen riders sifting quietly out the other end of the town.

The bastards had been there, all right. They had been planning to bust open the bank. But somehow they spotted the ambush and just melted away. A week later a bank in neighboring town was hit just before dawn and cleaned out completely. Two men who heard the explosion of the safe being blown and came out to see what was up lost their lives because of it.

That sheriff had been almighty pissed, but as far as he knew he never got a look at a White Hood. If he did, he sure didn't know about it at the time.

And now this bastard Markham was doing his level best to ensure that Custis Long never knowingly got a look at one of them either.

Longarm pressed his fingertips against his temples and rubbed, trying to take some of the pain away. "I'll tell you what," he said. "If you insist on playing this your way, with time running against us like it is, I'll just turn the whole case over to you and your deputies."

Markham blinked and looked pleased. Even Chief Deputy Mayes sat up straighter. The only one of them who didn't react was young Charlie Frye, and Longarm doubted that the boy was mature enough or bright enough to keep up with the conversation anyhow.

"You can have the tip," Longarm repeated, "and you can have the collar. Me, I'm out of the whole thing. Does that suit you, Sheriff?"

Markham glanced once at the big Colt Thunderer that rode at Longarm's waist. Longarm knew damned good and well what the man was thinking. Without at least one real lawman in the ambush party, old Markham himself might have to pick up a gun and appear on the scene. The shit-for-brains really didn't want to do that.

On the other hand, a successful ambush of the White Hoods—or an unsuccessful one, for that matter, so long as he was the man in sole charge of the glorious attempt—would almost guarantee him reelection to office.

"I am sorry you feel that way about it, Marshal, but I understand your position. I accept your withdrawal from the case, and I assure you I shall act on the information the Justice Department has conveyed to me. By nightfall, sir, this White Hood Gang shall be behind bars, and the streets

68

of Thunderbird Canyon shall be safe from depredation by..."

There was more to the line of bull, but Longarm was no longer listening. The case now belonged to Sheriff Paul S. Markham and his force of deputies.

Belonged to Sheriff Markham, that is, as far as Sheriff Markham knew.

"If you gentlemen would excuse me," Longarm said while the sheriff continued to natter on in a practice campaign speech, "I want to go over to the hotel and get some sleep now."

He set his Stetson gently onto an aching head and got the hell out of there.

Chapter 16

"You're the chief of security for Arrabie Minerals?"

"That's right," the big man said, giving Longarm a careful looking over. "You aren't here looking for work, not dressed like that you aren't, so what is it I can do for you?" He sounded suspicious.

Longarm smiled. Unlike Sheriff Paul Markham, this Jack Thomas looked like he had more between his ears than fried mush and bourbon whiskey.

Longarm closed the door behind him and helped himself to a seat in front of Thomas's desk.

Thomas was tall and broad-shouldered. The scars over his eyebrows and the lumpy shape of his nose said that he hadn't come up to his position as head of security for a large mining company by being someone's nephew, but there was intelligence in his eyes and a calm about him that implied confidence in his own abilities.

This was better, Longarm thought. He leaned forward and began to talk, laying out his badge and also the telegraph message from Arkansas as he spoke.

"Uh-oh," Thomas said when Longarm was done speaking. "Do you have any idea how much money is coming on that train this afternoon?"

Longarm shook his head. The lunacy with Paul Markham had never progressed far enough to think about information like that.

"I don't know how much the others are having shipped, of course, though I could take a guess. Our payroll alone, though, is more than fifteen thousand. Plus there's a payment due this month to the old boy who made the initial discovery here. He isn't so dumb as most of those backwoods prospectors. He cut a deal for royalties on top of a finder's fee, and it's paid to him every quarter. In cash. He insists on it. Says he doesn't trust bank drafts. I happen to know from worrying about the security that his payment this time will be over forty thousand. And with what should be coming to the other outfits"— Thomas whistled softly --"hell, Marshal, the total in that car should be in the neighborhood of seventy thousand dollars."

"That's serious money."

"Damn right it is," Thomas agreed.

"Fortunately it's being carried in a mail car. That makes it my business as well as yours, Jack."

"And glad I am for that, Marshal." The man paused and frowned. "Look, uh, Marshal Long—"

"Longarm," he corrected.

"Yeah, thanks. Okay, Longarm, it isn't really my place to say anything, but if you are counting much on the sheriff helping you with—"

"So I've discovered," Longarm interrupted. "No point in going into details now, but whatever I do next will be independent of your local authorities."

Thomas nodded and looked like he approved of that decision.

"For whatever it's worth, Marshal, you can count on the full cooperation of me and every one of my boys. We aren't a bunch of guntoughs or anything like that, but my people are all honest, decent men, and I'll vouch for each one of them. If I wasn't willing to say that about every last man of them, why, that man wouldn't be drawing pay from Arrabie."

"Good. I couldn't ask for more."

"And if you want to call in boys from the other mines, I'd have to say that they are every bit as good at the other outfits. We each have our own veins to follow, and any competition between us is the kind that you show in Fourth of July drilling contests and like that. There's nothing cut-throat between the mining companies here."

"Fine. But whatever we decide to do will have to be done on the quiet. I don't know if you've heard anything about these White Hoods, but—"

"I have. Too damn much, in fact."

"That simplifies things. They're a careful bunch, and we don't want to do anything to spook them. We'll have to set this up so nothing looks out of place." Longarm grinned. "And so the sheriff and his worthy deputies don't spot anything funny either."

Jack Thomas snorted with amusement. Apparently the picture did not have to be drawn any fuller than that for him to understand what Longarm was saying.

"You just tell me what you want, Longarm, and I'll make sure you have it."

"But on the quiet," Longarm said. "I have to think there's an inside connection here somewhere, or a bunch like the White Hoods wouldn't choose to take the train down at this end of the canyon. They have a good reason for what they're doing. They always do. So we have to keep it slow on who knows the truth."

"Speaking for my own boys, Longarm, they know better than to say anything out of school. For that matter, I can set them up one by one and put them where you want them, when you want them there, so that *they* won't know there's an operation in the works. They don't ask questions for the hell of it, and they know if there's anything I want to tell them I'll say it right out front. Otherwise, there'll be a reason for it and they won't balk. Now what is it you want me to do?"

Longarm knew the answer to that one readily enough. It was the plan he had worked out through the night and would have used with the local authorities if there had been any local authority in Thunderbird Canyon worth using.

He bent forward again and began to speak.

Jack Thomas began to smile when he was halfway through the idea, and by the time Longarm was done the

Arrabie security chief was grinning like a shit-eating possum.

"I take it you think it has possibilities," Longarm said when he was finished outlining his plan.

"Yeah," Thomas said with a chuckle. "I guess you could say that."

The big man pulled a watch from his vest pocket and checked the time. "Look," he said, "that train is due in an hour and a half. That's plenty of time for me to set up everything you want. And if you don't mind my saying so Longarm, you look like hell. I've got a cot in the back room for when things get busy. Why don't you stretch out on it for an hour while I tend to my play in this. I'll shake you out in plenty of time to be down at the depot."

"Jack, I can't remember when I've had a nicer offer. I'll take you up on that."

Thomas stood and reached for his hat. "By the time you wake up, Longarm, we'll have a surprise set and waiting for the gentlemen of the White Hood Gang."

Longarm yawned and grinned. Just thinking about a rest was enough to make him start feeling better. That and the impression of eager competence that Jack Thomas gave.

"I'll see you in an hour," Longarm said as Thomas departed.

Chapter 17

Jack Thomas had done his job mighty well. Or not at all. The point was, whichever of the depot loafers belonged to Thomas and Arrabie Minerals, Longarm couldn't spot them.

Sheriff Markham's crew was something else again. Enough to be laughable, really, if this weren't so damned serious.

Chief Deputy Roland Mayes was lurking inside the telegrapher's shack with a long-barrelled scattergun clutched in his hands and a lot of sweat beading his brow. Every few seconds he would peek out through a corner of the window and look at everybody else on the platform. The man looked like he was hoping the whole thing would go sour and the White Hoods not show up. The amazing thing to Longarm was that the man was still sober enough to find the window.

Deputy Charles Frye was a teenage gawker sitting barefoot and happy on the rim of one of the big ore hoppers extending out over the tracks where the Thunderbird Run would arrive. It wasn't something he had to pretend to be. The role fit him just fine. He still didn't have a weapon that Longarm could see, although maybe he had something tucked out of sight in the hopper. Either that or he was expected to chuck rocks at the White Hoods if and when they showed.

Thomas's people, though, were damned well hidden somewhere in the vicinity. Longarm did not go looking for them. The White Hoods were probably already among the other loafers on the platform.

There was the usual assortment of people waiting to meet the train. A man with a light, mule-driven spring wagon there to carry some expected package or cargo. A middle-aged couple who looked like they were going to greet someone due to arrive today. A drunk or two just come to see the sights.

The only group in evidence was a bunch of rowdy miners who were off shift but who still wore the grime and dust of a tour underground. The miners, there were ten or eleven of them, were half soused and waving bottles in the air, breaking out in song now and then, the words of which were making the woman half of the middle-aged couple blush. The delegation of miners were carrying a sign made out of a window shade nailed to a wooden slat. On the sign was painted *Welcome Fifi and Lola and the Girls*. There wasn't much doubt as to what they were so happy about.

Longarm gave up trying to figure out where Jack Thomas's boys were hiding—he did not want to be obvious about his interest in the question—and wondered instead whether the White Hoods were present.

With a sharp intake of breath and a narrowing of his eyes, he realized suddenly that the group of miners making such a show of meeting a passel of new whores were not all they seemed to be.

Once he paid attention to them, Longarm could see that the men were doing much waving of their bottles but not a hell of a lot of drinking from them.

Even those who were staggering and singing and seemingly drinking from their bottles were carrying bottles that remained full no matter how frequently the owners "drank."

And while not a single man carried a gun in sight, there were some suspiciously sagging coat pockets and not a few bulges where shoulder holsters might ride.

Son of a bitch, Longarm thought.

That crowd of so-called miners would be the White Hood Gang. Even the size of the bunch fit. He counted. Ten men.

It was them! It had to be!

Son of a *bitch!* It was all he could do to keep from dragging iron and throwing down on them right then and there. Instead, forcing himself to a calm he did not feel, he sauntered over to a bench under the covered platform and sat.

Far down the tracks he could see a plume of white smoke and hear the hollow, echoing sound of the train whistle announcing the arrival of the Thunderbird Run.

While he waited, the tiny locomotive coming into sight now, Longarm concentrated on memorizing the face of every man in that crowd of bogus rowdies. The bastards might wear hoods during their robberies, but right now they were playing the part of innocents, and every one of them had his bare face hanging out in the breeze.

Longarm took a last look around the platform—no sign of Sheriff Paul S. Markham, he noted in passing—and then once again bent to the study of those faces. Any of them who managed to get away today would be damn sure vulnerable tomorrow.

Because as far as everybody told him, there was no way out of the canyon except by rail. And if the least member of the White Hoods got away now, tonight the tracks would be guarded by Jack Thomas's boys, and tomorrow there wouldn't be a speck of dust leaving on the morning outbound until Custis Long had personally inspected the thing and given his approval for it to move to Meade Park.

This, by damn, was going to work.

Longarm leaned back on the bench and laced his hands over his stomach. The position looked innocent enough, but it also happened to put his right hand only inches from the butt of the big Colt in its crossdraw rig.

He should still have been tired, he knew, but right now he was so keyed-up and ready he did not care if he ever got a moment's sleep again.

Two hundred yards down the track the Thunderbird Run hooted, and the brakemen set the screws to bring the slow-moving train to a stop.

The mail car was the tender behind the wood car. It was close enough now that Longarm could see the open door behind which would be the safe containing a small fortune in hard cash. A man wearing sleeve garters and an eye-shade was leaning out of the doorway waving to someone.

Longarm tensed as the train shuddered and jolted to a stop practically in front of him.

Now!

Chapter 18

The middle-aged couple ambled down toward the end of the train where the passengers would disembark from the lone coach. Before they reached it a handsome girl in the kind of frock that almost had to be a school uniform got off and ran up the tracks to meet them with hugs and kisses.

The telegrapher came out of his shanty and went to the mail car to help unload.

Charlie Frye was flushed with nervous excitement. He bent to grab something out of the hopper behind him, lost his balance, and toppled down onto the load of ore waiting to be transferred into the rail cars.

The rowdies on the platform quit their make-believe drinking and sign waving and stood as if uncertain what to do next. What they *didn't* do was grab iron and head for the mail car. Nor did they pay any attention to the passenger coach end of the train, which was where any newly arriving whores would have been. In fact, none of them did very much except stand there.

There was no sign at all now of Chief Deputy Mayes. No peeping out of the window now. Nothing. The man had simply vanished once the train arrived.

The middle-aged couple and their pretty daughter linked arms and went walking happily into the center of town.

Jack Thomas stepped out of the telegrapher's shack and Longarm motioned to him

"Yeah?" Thomas asked.

Longarm leaned closer and whispered, "Alert your

boys, Jack. That must be the White Hoods right there with those phony signboards. Has to be them. Something's tipped them. We'll go ahead and take them now."

Thomas looked amused. "You got a charge to bring against them?"

"No, but . . . hell, I'll think of something. Jesus, Jack, we can jug 'em for loitering, or spitting on private property. Some damn thing. Then I'll see if I can't get a charge to stick later."

Charlie Frye climbed up onto the rim of the hopper again, this time holding a battered old percussion shotgun that had wire wrapped around the breech to keep the ancient thing from blowing up when it was fired. Or at least try and keep it from killing the shooter along with the intended victim. Frye looked dusty and disheveled after his swim in the crushed silver ore.

"Uh, I kinda hate to tell you this, Longarm," Thomas said with poorly concealed humor.

"What's that?"

"Those people you're wanting to arrest?"

"Yeah?"

"I can't call my boys to take them in, Longarm."

"Why the hell not?"

"Longarm." Thomas grinned now. "Those *are* my boys. I, uh, figured I'd hide 'em in plain sight."

"Aw . . . shit!" If Longarm had had something in his hands to throw he damn sure would have thrown it. "So where are the fucking White Hoods?"

Jack Thomas shrugged. "Beats the hell outa me, Longarm. There isn't a man on this platform that I haven't known for at least the past year and a half. The only stranger I see anywhere around here is you. And I don't guess you're the damn White Hood Gang all by yourself." He snickered. "By the way," he added, "you know our good sheriff's chief deputy?"

"Sure."

"I just left him in the shack there. He's all huddled up in a corner looking ready to puke from being scared so bad."

"Well, tough shit," Longarm complained.

"Yeah," Thomas agreed. "Look, why don't we go over and help unload the payroll shipment. What I think is that we better put it all under guard tonight until the disbursements tomorrow. Just in case your White Hoods are still hanging around wanting the stuff."

Longarm nodded. "I agree. We don't know what scared them off this afternoon, but whatever it was, there's no guarantee they won't make a try for it yet." He sighed. "My hopes sure were high, though, Jack."

"I know what you mean, Longarm. I know what you mean." The two men walked toward the mail car, where the mail clerk was taking sacks of coin out of the safe and dropping them at the doorway for Thomas's people—who by now had quit their drunken-miner act—to carry off to the small, stone-walled building that served Thunderbird Canyon as a bank.

Charlie Frye crawled down off the ore hopper and lent a hand. There still was no sign of either Roland Mayes or Paul Markham.

Chapter 19

Now that the nervous energy of anticipation had all come crashing down into the despair of futility, Longarm felt like he was ready to collapse.

It was Friday afternoon and he'd had . . . what? . . . two or three hours of sleep since he woke up in Morey and Eugenie Fahnwell's guest room on Wednesday morning.

Lances of sharp pain were shooting through his head from sheer fatigue, and he felt fuzzy and groggy-minded, like a man coming off a ten-day drunk. This wasn't his idea of a fun time, and there was still some work to be done before he could find a bed to drop into.

Sheriff Markham and Chief Deputy Mayes put in an appearance in time to oversee the transfer of the payroll shipment to the bank. Obviously both men thought it safe now to appear on the streets again. Neither of them commented on their conspicuous absence when the White Hoods were supposed to hit.

If the idiots wanted to take charge and act tough now, Longarm decided, let them. The ambush was blown anyway. And, thank goodness, Thunderbird Canyon's petty political problems were no worry of his. All Longarm wanted right now was to clear up a few other matters and get the hell gone on the first available train.

He followed the crowd to the bank and watched while the money—$72,319 in gold coin and a little silver for the small change—was placed into the cheese-box vault of mild steel.

"Chief Deputy Mayes will take the first watch tonight," Markham said in an officious manner. "Deputy Frye will relieve him at midnight."

"With this much money at stake," Thomas suggested, "I think it would be a good idea if some of our security people assisted your men, Sheriff."

"Excellent idea, Mr. Thomas. I accept," Markham declared.

Interesting, Longarm thought, because it pretty much proved that Jack Thomas was not the man Paul Markham was fretting about come election time. Longarm was certain Markham was the kind of small-minded fool who would never accept even a perfect idea from an enemy. Not even if he could turn it to his own advantage. That seemed rather a pity for the town's sake. Jack Thomas was twice the leader that Paul Markham could ever hope to be.

"You men don't need me, then," Longarm said.

Markham ignored him, but Thomas said, "Lord, no, Longarm. You look like lukewarm death on the hoof. Go bunk out. If anything happens, I'll call you."

"Good enough."

Longarm left the bank, but instead of turning toward the hotel and the much-needed bed that was waiting for him there, he climbed laboriously and painfully to the next street level, up the steep hill and down the narrow street toward Jessie's Place. There was a certain pleasure he wanted to tend to there before he took time out for sleep.

"Mr. Long, isn't it? Come in, please." Jessie herself greeted him at the door, although it was early for normal business hours.

Even so, the place was busy enough, with a half a dozen girls—all of them young, all of them Mexican, all of them attractive—already in the parlor. There was one customer already there examining the choices before him, an elderly, balding man with a large belly and expensive clothing.

"And what is your pleasure this afternoon, Mr. Long?

Would you like to visit with Rosalie again? Or perhaps one of our other young ladies would . . ."

She turned away from him, leading him toward the parlor and the other occupants of the place.

Longarm was not really listening to the bitch's sales pitch. He stepped up close behind her and took her hand.

Jessie stopped and gave him an inquiring look.

"Ah, Miss Jessie, a pleasure this will be, I assure you."

She raised an eyebrow.

Grinning, Longarm pulled his handcuffs out and snapped one bracelet onto her wrist.

"Really, Mr. Long, I . . ."

He wrenched her other arm behind her and applied the second cuff.

"Mr. Long," she protested, "I realize you are new to our services. And this sort of thing is perfectly appropriate with any of the girls you choose. But really, sir, I do not personally engage in . . ."

Still grinning, he took out his wallet and flipped it open to display his badge.

"Like I said, ma'am. A pleasure. Truly a pleasure."

Jessie was calm enough about it. She bent slightly to examine the badge, and he held it higher for her convenience. She looked it over carefully, then her mouth twisted into a sneer. She did not look at all perturbed.

"You fool," she spat. "Don't you know that prostitution is subject to local law, not federal? As you may have already discovered, sir, I have no problems with the local law. Now release me at once, or I shall become quite angry with you."

Longarm continued to grin. "As you have already discovered, madam, I am not local law. And the way I understand it, slavery *is* a federal offense. I am arresting you for the crime of slaving, which is prohibited by whatever the hell amendment to the constitution."

"You cocksucker!" the lovely Miss Jessie hissed.

"No, ma'am. Nor slaver neither." He was still grinning.

"This is ridiculous," she yelped, looking worried now for the first time. "Let me go at once, I tell you."

"Miss Jessie, if a judge decides that I'm ridiculous, then I expect I'll believe it. Meantime, madam, you will sit in a jail cell awaiting that judge's pleasure." He tugged on the handcuffs, pulling her toward the front door.

"Where do you think you are taking me?" she demanded. Her voice had risen and become shrill.

"Denver," he said bluntly. "Federal court in Denver."

Jessie jerked free of his grip, the effort undoubtedly painful when the manacles cut into her wrists, and shrieked, "Walter!"

She did not try to run but threw herself forward onto the floor, twisting sideways to avoid striking the rich, plush carpet face first.

Longarm looked up and saw a bouncer peering back at him.

The bouncer was not a large man. In fact, he was probably not as tall or as heavily built as the woman who employed him. He was a smallish, slightly built man with the facial features of a sewer rat and stringy hair that covered only the right side of his head. His menace did not lie in his size but in the size of the large-bore, double-barreled shotgun he was holding steady in the direction of Longarm's stomach.

Longarm cursed himself. If he hadn't been so damned tired. . . . But that was only making excuses.

"Shuck the hardware," Walter ordered.

Longarm looked into the big bores of the shotgun but hesitated.

Walter smiled at him. "I've killed bigger men than you, mister."

"It's Marshal, not mister," Longarm corrected. "United States Deputy Marshal Custis Long out of Denver."

"Big fucking deal. So this time I'll blow a marshal's guts out. I never done that before." The smile got wider. "Might be fun, now that I think on it."

Well, it had been worth a try, Longarm thought ruefully.

"Now which will it be, federal Deputy Marshal? Do you wanna shuck the gun, or would you rather we pick you up with a mop?"

"Given the choice," Longarm said, "I expect I'll lose the gun."

"Very sensible," Walter said.

Jessie was lying on the floor giving Longarm a look of very ugly triumph.

Sensible shit, Longarm realized. Once they had him there was no way they were going to turn him loose to try again. Still...

He held his right hand far from his body and with his left unbuckled the gunbelt at his waist. "Easy now," he said softly. "I won't try any tricks."

The holstered Colt slithered over his hips as soon as the buckle was loose and landed on the carpet with a solid thump.

"That's better," Walter said.

Without waiting to be told, Longarm used the toe of his boot to flip the gunbelt and Colt well out of reach. Then he leaned forward and extended a hand to Jessie.

"May I help you up, madam?"

The look in her eyes was murderous. "Get these things off of me," she demanded.

"Yes, ma'am," Longarm answered in as meek a voice as he could manage.

He stepped up behind her and dipped two fingers into his vest pocket.

Chapter 20

It wasn't a handcuff key that Longarm kept brazed to the end of his watch chain, but a .41 caliber rimfire derringer. The tiny palmful of death came into his hand as he stepped up behind Jessie.

Longarm grabbed her throat with his left hand, holding her between him and the menace of Walter's shotgun, and the cold muzzle of the little derringer snugged tightly into the hollow beneath her right ear.

Jessie yelped and tried to pull away but, handcuffed and held firmly, she had no chance.

"This isn't the gentlemanly thing to do, I realize," Longarm said calmly, "but I think now it's your turn to shuck the iron, Walter. Or the only way to take me is to take your boss first."

Walter laughed. It sounded more like a bark.

Jessie's eyes got wide, and she began to tremble.

"Do what he says, Walter. Do what he says at once!"

By now they had begun to attract the attention of the guest in the parlor, staring wild-eyed and frightened at the scene being played out in the foyer, and the Mexican working girls looking on with dull-eyed disinterest. The captive whores, playthings of anyone with money enough to pay for the privilege of abusing them, acted like they had seen so much already that they had seen it all. As if nothing that could possibly happen in this house would concern them anymore.

"I really think you should do what the lady says," Longarm suggested. "Just lay the shotgun down. Nice and easy so it doesn't go off by accident and hurt somebody. Then we'll work things out, and nobody gets hurt."

Walter laughed again.

Longarm did not particularly like the sound of that.

"Do it, Walter. He'll shoot me. I know he will." Jessie was in a state of agitation that had her sweating and stuttering. It completely ruined Longarm's image of her as the high-toned lady of breeding and quality that she presented herself to be.

"Lay the gun down now," Longarm urged.

"Shit, mister, you think that bitch can't be replaced? Easy as pie, mister," Walter said. "The boss can hire all o' them he wants. A snap o' the finger and they'll be lined up at the door wanting to hire on as madam o' this gold mine." Walter grinned. "No, the way I see it, mister, I'll just take the both of you. No more problems then. See?"

He lifted the lethal shotgun to his shoulder.

Well *shit*. Longarm thought. This was not going at all the way it was supposed to.

On the surface of things his choices seemed simple enough. He could stand there and let Walter shoot him and Jessie with one load of buck. Or he could set the derringer aside and allow Walter to shoot him more conveniently out of the sight and hearing of the witnesses in the parlor. Some choices.

"You win," he said quickly, and Walter's finger relaxed on the double triggers of the scattergun. To Jessie he added, "Sorry, madam. I didn't actually mean for any harm to come to you."

"You son of a bitch!" the ungrateful whore snapped. "Sorry! Sorry, is it?" She tried to kick him, raking his right shin painfully with the heel of her shoe.

Walter was laughing again, obviously enjoying Longarm's discomfort and Jessie's anger.

Longarm shrugged and winked at the man—then twisted the little derringer and shot Walter in the face.

Since threatening Jessie hadn't done it, he had to take the only other route open to him.

The brutal little pistol bellowed, twisting sideways in Longarm's hand from the poorly contained recoil. A bloody dimple appeared on Walter's upper lip as the heavy slug from the tiny gun plowed into his half-open mouth and on through tissue and bone, sweeping teeth and scraps of vertebrae with it.

Walter went pale and sat down abruptly, his legs folding so suddenly that they dropped him straight down into a cross-legged position against the foyer wall.

Much too late to do him any good, his finger contracted involuntarily on the rear trigger of the shotgun, and a flaming eruption of lead pellets tore a swath of destruction through the carpet and floorboards of the fancy house.

The recoil of the shot shell kicked the gun loose from Walter's nerveless fingers, and the stock bounded up to hit him a glancing blow across the temple.

Longarm pushed Jessie away from him and jumped forward to retrieve the shotgun before Walter could get his sense back and reach for it. One barrel of the weapon remained loaded, and Walter was still alive.

The man looked at Longarm with blank, uncomprehending eyes. He worked his mouth trying to speak, but no words came out. The best he could do was a croaking hiss of moving air. The entire roof of his mouth was torn away, and there was a hole in the back of his neck big enough to accomodate a bird's nest. Blood was pumping out of his mouth and out of the wound in his neck. Lots of blood. He had only a minute or two left before the loss of blood would kill him.

"My God, he's still alive?" Jessie was lying on the torn carpet of the foyer floor, hands still cuffed behind her.

"Yeah. Crazy what the human body can take, ain't it."

"He's bleeding. You've got to stop him from bleeding."

"What the hell d'you want me to do, tie a tourniquet around his neck an' hang him instead?"

88

"Fine, but make him quit bleeding all over my rug. Do you know how much that thing cost?"

Nice folks at Jessie's Place, Longarm thought sourly. He snapped open the breach of the shotgun and dropped both shells, the live one and the empty one, onto the now bloody carpet, then tossed the gun aside. He went over to the parlor entry and retreived his Colt and gunbelt. He felt much better with that around his waist again.

Walter solved Jessie's immediate fears by dying before the carpet was beyond cleaning. He remained sitting upright, propped against the wall with his eyes open but unseeing. The flow of blood dropped off to a slow ooze and then stopped altogether.

"Decent of you, Walter," Longarm muttered.

The elderly customer with the big belly and the newly chalky complexion fumbled for his hat, paused long enough to throw up violently into the lap of the girl he had been stroking a few minutes earlier, and disappeared in a surprisingly agile run toward the back of the place. Longarm suspected he would not be seeing the gentleman again.

The Mexican girls sat where they were, but he thought he could see a flicker of interest in them now that Walter was dead and Jessie still in handcuffs.

"The party's almost over, girls," Longarm told them. "I want you all to go to your rooms and wait there. You don't have to worry about anyone hurting you again, though. The government will feed and house you till the trial is over, and then we'll see that you get home again."

Most of the girls acted like they did not really understand, but one of them actually smiled. She began talking in rapid-fire Spanish to the rest of them.

On the floor near Longarm's boots, Jessie tried to struggle onto her feet, failed, and had to settle for a sitting position, which was the best she could manage with her hands cuffed.

"Mr. Long . . . Marshal . . . we can talk this over. Be reasonable. There really doesn't *have* to be a trial, you know."

She was trying to give him an enticing, come-hither smile, but she could not quite pull it off.

"Normally I'd agree," Longarm said. "It'd be a lot less expensive for the taxpayers if I just turned you over to the girls."

Jessie blanched a fish-belly white at *that* thought.

"But as it happens, ma'am," Longarm went on as if he hadn't noticed, "I expect we'll need your testimony to nail the owner of this place. Seeing as how it isn't really you." He smiled down at her.

The lovely Miss Jessie was ready to cling to the straws Longarm was holding within her grasp now. She gave him another of those sickly smiles and said, "You'll tell the judge that I cooperated, won't you?"

"Kinda depends on whether or not you cooperate, doesn't it?"

"Help me up, dearie. There are some papers in my office I'd like to show you."

"Very nice of you to volunteer," he said. He bent and helped her to her feet.

Behind them the captive whores were huddled together, talking excitedly. Some of them were beginning to believe it now. They were laughing and crying at the same time.

"Don't forget," Longarm told them, "I'll need your help here. But I'll see that you are comfortable, and we'll get you home again just as soon as possible."

Then he took Jessie by the elbow and led the woman into the small but richly-furnished office where all the lovely records were kept.

Funny thing, but he didn't feel nearly as exhausted now as he had just a little while ago.

Chapter 21

Longarm climbed the stairs to the top floor of the courthouse slowly. He was tired again—Lord, but he was tired. His head was throbbing, and his eyes felt like they were on fire. But he was satisfied. For all of that he was satisfied.

Jessie came willingly enough with him. She had recovered her composure and now was almost optimistic about it all.

"You'll be sure to tell the judge how helpful I've been?" she had asked over and over again. It seemed that she was finally willing to believe that he would, and that therefore her troubles with the law would only be minor, temporary discomfortures and nothing involving years without makeup or champagne.

"Ever been up here before?" he asked when they reached the top landing.

Jessie gave him a dirty look.

"Of course you haven't. How silly of me to ask," Longarm said.

He pushed open the door to the sheriff's office and took Jessie by the elbow to escort her inside. She was, of course, still handcuffed.

There was no sign of the chief deputy or of Charlie Frye. Those worthy gentlemen should either be guarding the bank vault or sleeping, getting ready to guard the vault when the other went off duty.

The office was occupied, though, by Sheriff Paul Markham and two handsomely-dressed older gentlemen. Markham had a bottle and glasses set out on his desk and was holding forth with a look of importance when Longarm and Jessie walked in on the trio.

"Ah, gentlemen, here is the deputy marshal who conveyed the tip to me." If he noticed Jessie—and how the hell could he not—he made no mention of her. "Deputy Long, isn't it?" He blinked owlishly and took a drink. The bottle on the desk this evening had a much finer label than the one Markham had shared the night before, Longarm noted.

With an airy, self-important wave, Markham introduced his guests as major stockholders in the two larger mines in Thunderbird Canyon.

"Yes," one of them said, "we were just telling Paul how appreciative we are of him and his deputies running off the White Hood Gang like that. Outstanding work, of course. Quite outstanding."

"It was?" Longarm asked.

"Oh my, yes. Saved our payrolls, didn't he? Of course he did. Outstanding work, that." The gentleman—Longarm had not quite caught the slurred name when Markham gave it—was well along toward being in his cups.

Longarm had to smile. Simply had to. And to give appropriate credit to Sheriff Paul Markham. Indeed, defeat had been transformed into a victory of the most sterling quality. Now it wasn't so much that the whole bunch of them had stood around on the railroad platform with their thumbs up their butts waiting for something that never happened. Now it was that the skill and determination of Sheriff Paul S. Markham so frightened the White Hood Gang that the gang members fled trembling into the distance, while the lives and property of the Thunderbird Canyon mines were secured for all time.

Or something like that.

It was all pure bullshit politics, of course, but hell, Longarm could admire that too when it was so beautifully done. Definitely a case of credit where credit was due. Why, with something like this behind him and the full support and approval of the men who paid out those salvaged payrolls, good old Paul could probably count on re-election for years to come. Or until the ore veins pinched out, whichever came first.

Longarm smiled and touched the brim of his Stetson to Markham in honest admiration of the man's peculiar abilities.

"Was there something you wanted to see me about, Deputy?" Markham asked importantly, still ignoring Jessie.

"Yes, I need to use two of your cells for some federal prisoners, Sheriff."

"Really? Found some of those White Hoods, did you? Good work, Long. I shall forward a recommendation to your chief. Good work, man." Markham had another drink and leaned forward to tilt the bottle over the mine owner's glasses as well.

Longarm coughed into his fist. "Actually, Sheriff, these prisoners concern another case. You know how that is. You start out looking for one thing and find another." He shrugged as if in apology.

"Of course, man. How well I understand. Still, good work regardless. Just bring your men in, and I shall be glad to allow you the use of my cells."

He managed to act like he was in charge of a large prison the way he said it, though in fact there were only three small cells built across the back wall of the office space the sheriff had been given.

"Matter of fact," Longarm drawled, "this is one of my prisoners here." He pointed, and this time Markham was forced to concede that there was a madam in his office.

"Really now, Long. Surely you are mistaken here." He shot a nervous glance toward his two distinguished guests, and Longarm suspected that Markham was struggling with the question of whether he wanted to raise a jurisdiction dispute—one that he did not yet know the ground ru to—in front of those politically powerful gentlemen.

As Longarm had expected, Markham settled fo

dence and did not raise the point that whoring was not a federal crime.

"Whatever," he said smoothly. "No skin off my back, eh?" He tossed the cell keys to Longarm and gave his visitors a smile.

Longarm led Jessie into the cell on the left end of the short row, removed the handcuffs, and helped her to a seat on the bare cot. "I'll see if we can't rustle up some comforts later," he told her.

She nodded, looking unhappy again now that she was actually looking at the world through steel bars. She had been cheerful enough for a while, but now all that belief that things would once again be rosy deserted her and she looked pale and drawn.

"It won't be so bad," he said, not really sure if that was the truth or not. "Not bad" for a spectator might be pure hell for the recipient of a prison sentence. It all depended on the viewpoint of the man or woman who happened to be in the jug.

On the other hand, Jessie had come up through the ranks of whoredom to become a madam. Whatever happened to her after Longarm turned her over to the matrons in Denver, she had probably already had worse.

He returned his handcuff key to his pocket and left Jessie in the cell, closing and carefully locking the door on her. She did not look up, and seemed to be in a state of mild shock now that the bars were actually surrounding her.

"Pity," one of the mine owners said when Longarm rejoined them. "Hate to see a woman in irons. What'd she do?"

"The charge is slavery," Longarm told him.

"Really? I thought that was all over with. Besides, I ven't seen a nigra here since last summer."

"Wasn't blacks she bought," Longarm told him. "Mexi-Girls, as a matter of fact."

"Really? Not so many of them around town neither. Humph!"

"No, I don't expect you'd have seen any of them unless you visited a certain house in town."

"What? Oh. Not I, sir. Not I. Never visited one of those places, sir, nor wallowed in a sty with the hogs. Same difference, sir. Same difference exactly." He harrumphed loudly again and had a drink of Markham's whiskey.

Longarm noticed that neither Markham nor the other gentleman made declarations about how far above such dealings they were. And neither pretended never to have seen Jessie before. Neither admitted to it, of course, they simply remained silent on the question.

"We'll be moving on to our dinner shortly, Long," Markham said like a man who wanted a subject changed. "Don't be long about fetching in the other felon, will you? Office might be closed if you tarry."

"Oh, there won't be any delay at all, Sheriff," Longarm said politely.

He was still holding the handcuffs he had removed from Jessie. When Markham reached for his glass, Longarm flipped one of the bracelets over the sheriff's wrist.

"Here now, what's this! I'm in no mood for playfulness. Long."

Longarm smiled and, hauling Markham's hands behind his back, snapped the other cuff in place.

"Have you lost your senses, man?"

Longarm reached inside his coat and produced a thin sheaf of documents that had been folded to fit a pocket. "Evidence," he said. "Deed to certain property. Employment agreement. Even, Sheriff, a certain record of payment to a Chief Josephino Nana'a for three captive females. Damned stupid of you to keep such accurate accounts, Sheriff. But I do appreciate it." To the startled mine owners Longarm added, "It seems the good sheriff here has been feathering his nest with human flesh, gentlemen. The Apaches would steal Mexican women, and the

sheriff would buy them. But not to give them their free-
dom. He bought 'em and rented them out to any bastard
with some loot in his pockets."

He peeled one of the documents out of the bunch and
held it for the gentlemen to see.

"This one is a record of a purchase made through a man
known as Daniels. I expect this Daniels will be on our
wanted list directly. Your good sheriff here bought a
thirteen-year-old girl named Maria, and a seventeen-year-
old named Concepcion for twelve Kennedy repeating rifles
and half a case of .45-60 ammunition." Longarm winked at
Markham. "Naturally we'll want to see if you and this
Daniels fella had a trader's license. If you didn't, Sheriff,
there may be some other federal charges for you to answer."

The man who had been quiet stayed that way, but the
one who was too dignified to hump whores looked like he
was about to have a stroke. He slapped his whiskey glass
back onto Markham's desk like he thought the thing was
contaminated.

"Really!"

"Yeah," Longarm agreed pleasantly. "Really and truly."

The man stood, stuffed his chin high into the air, and
marched out of the office without a backward glance for
his dishonored "friend."

The other one at least had the good grace to give Markham a sympathetic shrug. Then he too left. Longarm could
hear their shoe soles thumping on the staircase.

"I think you don't have many friends here anymore,
Paul."

Markham did not answer. He looked too shattered to
speak or even to hear now.

Longarm took him by the arm and led him to the second
borrowed cell. He cuffed the sheriff to one of his own cell
bars, just in case Mayes or Frye should return and want to
ʳee their boss, and locked him securely inside the cell

before he dropped the keys into his coat pocket and left the two prisoners to themselves.

It was over now, all of it, and Longarm's ass was truly dragging as he stumbled into the street in front of the courthouse and turned toward the hotel.

Chapter 22

"Whu—?"

Longarm snapped from deep sleep straight into action, his hand sweeping for the Colt no amount of fatigue could keep him from having positioned by his head before he went to bed.

"Easy, sir, it's only me."

Longarm blinked, the big Thunderer already pointing toward the intruder almost before he realized that he was not alone in the hotel room, and recognized Charlie Frye holding a glass-globed lamp and looking ready to run for it at the sight of the .45.

"Oh. It's you." He sat up, running his palm over eyes that had not yet had near enough sleep. Anger replaced the sense of groggy unreality, and his jaw firmed as he shoved the Colt back into its holster. "What the fuck are you doing waking me up in the middle of the night?"

"It's just past eleven, sir," young Frye said, as if Longarm gave a crap what time it was. "And . . . and there's trouble, sir. Big trouble. I thought I should wake you."

"Well, you've done that for damn sure." Longarm was still feeling more peeved than concerned. Damn these locals anyhow. He swung his legs off the side of the bed and reached for a cheroot and a match. "Now what is so important that it couldn't wait till morning?"

"The . . . the bank's been blown up, sir. There's all kinds ole dead. And I can't seem to find the sheriff, sir. I ght . . ."

"The sheriff is in one of his own cells, damnit, right there in his own office, and..." Longarm jerked, fully awake now for the first time. "You said *what*?"

Young Deputy Frye fussed nervously with the lamp and swayed from one foot to the other. "I...I said the bank was blowed up, Marshal."

"Blown up?"

Frye nodded miserably. "Just a bit ago. There was... there was Chief Deputy Mayes in there guarding. And Mr. Jack Thomas from the Arrabie, he was there too. An' a guard from Tyler Mining an' another man from the Huckman mine. It's a mess, Marshal. They're dead. All of 'em dead. Blowed 'most apart, they are."

Longarm felt a sinking feeling in his stomach. "What about the money?"

"Just what you'd expect, Marshal. The vault, what's left of it, is empty as empty can be."

Longarm stood and reached for his clothes. There would be time enough for sleep sometime, but that time was not now.

"You was saying that Sheriff Markham was s'posed to be in a cell, Marshal?"

"That's right," Longarm said while he stepped into his trousers and stamped his feet into his boots. He expected Frye to ask why the sheriff should be in one of his own cells.

Instead, the young deputy said, "I was just over to the office, Marshal. That's the second place I looked for the sheriff. But there wasn't nobody there, sir. Just the night lamp burnin' and all the cell doors standing empty."

Longarm felt ready to spit and start screaming.

Was there any other damn thing that could go wrong tonight?

The one thing, the only thing, that Longarm felt absolutely certain about right now was that if there *was* anything else that could fuck up, it *would*.

He finished dressing and followed Deputy Charlie Frye out into the night.

Chapter 23

Half the population of Thunderbird Canyon, everybody who wasn't on shift underground, seemed to be gathered around what was left of the bank building.

A few were engaged in pulling the rubble away from the ruins. The others seemed interested in seeing how far they could exaggerate the latest rumor but still allow the tale to remain remotely believable. Longarm ignored the bystanders and pushed his way through to the heap of rock that had been a building.

The bank had been a narrow, two-story affair constructed of native stone. Now both floors were occupying a single, ground-level space. Several blanket-covered bodies were laid out on the ground nearby. Longarm checked. One of them had been Chief Deputy Mayes. The other man he did not recognize.

"Who did you tell me was dead, Deputy?" he asked Frye, who was still trailing at Longarm's elbow with a helplessly lost expression on his beardless face.

"There was the chief deputy, like you see there, an' Long Louie, that's him lying there, and Mr. Thomas, and a fella from the Huckman." Frye thought for a moment, then nodded. "I think that's everybody."

"Where are the other bodies?" Longarm asked.

Frye pointed to the mound of rock. "Under there someplace, I reckon."

"But how do you know who was in the building, and who died, if the bodies haven't been recovered yet?"

"Oh. I was there just five, ten minutes before the thing blew up, Marshal. I got me some sleep an' woke up a bit ago and come by to see if the chief deputy wanted to be relieved early. I seen everybody then, but the chief deputy tol' me to go get some breakfast before I took over the guardin'." Frye shuddered. "If he hadn't sent me off t' eat . . ."

Longarm could understand the young man's distress, of course. Frye could easily have been inside the bank when the explosion ripped it apart. Right now, though, Longarm needed information more than Frye needed sympathy. "You also said the bank vault is empty, Charlie. How would anybody know that?" Longarm pressed.

The deputy pointed toward a back corner of the mess. "Over there, Marshal. The top of the vault's sticking up outa the flooring from upstairs. C'mon, and I'll show you."

Frye led as they picked their way over loose rubble and timber, the way lighted by a hundred lanterns hastily brought by the men who were looking for possible survivors. Everyone knew there was no chance of finding anyone still alive under all that rock, but the miners were making the effort every bit as seriously as they would have tried to rescue comrades trapped by a cave-in underground. This sort of thing was something they had more experience with than any of them likely wanted.

As they reached the back of the bank building Longarm could see the flat steel top of the old vault protruding from a pile of floorboards and filth. The ornately decorated door, painted in gold scrollwork, stuck up ten or eleven inches out of the pile. It was easy to see at a glance that the door was partially open. Longarm called for a lantern, and one was handed to him. He leaned forward and directed the light inside the vault as best he could.

Young Frye had been right about that, at least. The floor of the vault was littered with dust and fallen papers, but there was no sign of the bags of cash that had been deposited there earlier in the afternoon.

"Son of a ..." Longarm started to mutter. He was interrupted by a flurry of excited voices from his right.

"Over here," someone was calling. "We found another over here."

Longarm and Frye and half a hundred other men pushed toward the sound of the voice.

Three burly men in overalls and narrow-brimmed hats were straining to lift a beam that once offered support to the bank's roof. Before Longarm could reach them, a dozen more men jumped forward to put their muscle into the effort, and the beam was slowly raised inch by painful inch.

Without waiting for a prop to be brought, another man dropped belly-down and edged forward quickly until his head and shoulders were beneath the awful weight of the beam. He was trusting his life to the men doing the lifting. If they slipped, if the beam were allowed to fall, the rescuer would be snuffed out like a candle in a windstorm.

"I got him!" the courageous rescuer shouted. "I got 'im. Pull me out."

More volunteers grasped the rescuer by the ankles while above him the men straining to hold the beam aloft sweated and grew red-faced from their sustained effort.

Longarm and the other men who were gathered close could see that the rescuer had hold of a man's wrist. The others hauled backward, pulling rescuer and victim alike out from under the ominous weight of the heavy beam. As they were pulled clear, though, the rescuer's face went white and he relased his grip on the wrist they all could see.

He let go and scrambled backward on his own, jerking away from the surprised and confused men who had been helping him. He rolled out away from the men who were holding up the beam and turned on hands and knees to vomit. Then, wiping his mouth with the back of a wrist, he shook his head and said, "Let 'er down, boys. Just let it drop."

"But—"

"Damnit," the rescuer said in an anguished voice, "leave be."

"But we seen—"

"'Twasn't a man," the rescuer spat. "'Twas just an arm and shoulder."

"Jesus," someone said.

Someone else stepped forward and offered the rescuer a pint bottle. The man drank from it deeply and gratefully, threw up again, and drank a second time.

"That looked like Mr. Thomas's shirt," Frye said quietly.

Longarm grunted. He touched Frye's elbow and motioned for the boy to follow. Slowly he led the way out of the rubble and past the throngs of spectators on the street. There was no point in waiting there any longer. He had seen what he had to. And it could take the night and perhaps several more days before all the mess was cleaned away and the bodies recovered. The silver miners of Thunderbird Canyon were better able to accomplish that job than Longarm, anyway.

"Yes, sir?" Frye asked when they were clear of the crowd.

"You also told me, didn't you, that you'd been up to the jail and there wasn't anybody there?"

"Yes, sir, that's right. First place I looked was at Miss Jessie's place. The sheriff, he likes to go there of an evening. But it was closed for some reason tonight, so I went to the jail. Like I told you, the night lamp was burning but there wasn't nobody there."

Longarm cursed some more. He had left Jessie and Paul Markham both behind bars, damnit, and Markham handcuffed to a cell bar for good measure.

"You didn't let anyone out of the cells there?" Longarm asked Frye.

"Sir?" The young deputy looked genuinely confused. "I don't know how you'd mean, sir. The cells was empty Wasn't anybody in them to let out even if I'd wanted Which o' course I wouldn't."

"Yeah. Sure."

Longarm climbed to the top floor of the courthouse anyway. Frye had been telling the truth. The office and cells were empty. A lamp with the wick trimmed low burned in a wall fixture.

The only thing Longarm could see out of place—except of course for the cell doors that were standing open—was a desk drawer that was slightly ajar. He was fairly sure that that drawer had been closed when he left the room earlier.

Longarm pulled the drawer open. It held a few papers, an ink bottle, and a tray of steel pen nibs, nothing of real interest. "What did Markham keep in here, Charlie?"

Frye glanced over his shoulder. "Just the stuff you see there, Marshal, and I think some spare sets of keys too. I don't see them, though."

"Handcuff keys?"

"Sure." Frye's expression showed that he had no idea what Longarm was getting at. Longarm was convinced the youngster was not actor enough to play this out as a role. He honestly did not know what, if anything, could be wrong here.

"Sit down, Charlie. I think it's about time I told you a few things. Like for instance how I guess you are the acting sheriff here now that Chief Deputy Mayes is dead."

Charlie blinked in confusion but sat where he was told.

Longarm found Markham's whiskey in a bottom desk drawer, selected the better of the two labels available there, and poured drinks for both of them. He didn't know about Charlie Frye, but right about now Longarm felt a need for a stout drink.

"Now, Charlie, the situation is . . ."

Chapter 24

It was three o'clock in the morning, undoubtedly an odd time for the county's board of supervisors to meet, but Longarm had insisted on having the three men brought together at this hour.

Two of the men he had already met. They had been Paul Markham's distinguished visitors the evening before, when Longarm broke up Markham's party by putting the sheriff under arrest. The tall gentleman who was too dignified to consort with whores turned out to the S. Vance Hightower, his companion the previous evening Wellington Jones, and the third supervisor Howie Bright. Among them they represented major ownership interests in the three mines of Thunderbird Canyon—damn convenient, Longarm thought, for the big money to represent all the local political power too—and Jones owned the Huckman mine outright.

All of them had been awake in the aftermath of the bank explosion, but none seemed particularly pleased to be called into emergency session now. Charlie Frye sat meekly off in a corner looking nervous and more than a little afraid.

"Thank you for coming, gentlemen," Longarm told them.

"Better be a damned good reason for this, Marshal," Bright said.

"There is, sir." Longarm cleared his throat and reached for a cheroot. Fatigue was making his head ache and thump again, and a shot of rye would have been much more welcome than a smoke right now, but this was not the time for it. Later would have to do.

"As I am sure you are all aware, gentlemen, Thunderbird Canyon is having a difficult night."

"That's one way of putting it," Bright agreed.

"To belabor the obvious, gentlemen, your bank has been blown up and your payroll funds stolen, presumably by the White Hood Gang. At the same time, your sheriff, under arrest for violation of federal antislavery laws, has managed an escape from custody and has disappeared."

"So we're told," Bright said sourly.

"The point is, gentlemen, this is a moment of crisis. What I need from you is a formal declaration of emergency."

"Toward what end, Marshal?" Hightower asked.

"If you declare a state of emergency, and request official assistance from the federal government, I will be empowered to step in and take whatever emergency measures I deem necessary. Without that declaration, I'm afraid I won't be able to help seek the men who dynamited your bank and stole more than seventy thousand dollars from you."

"You won't?"

Longarm shook his head. "I was assigned to this case on the basis of a tip that said the payroll was to be stolen from a mail car on a chartered railroad, gentlemen. Theft from the mails is a federal crime, and it was within my jurisdiction to block that if I could. As we all know, that planned crime did not take place. The money was transferred out of the mail car without incident and deposited in your local bank. Correct me if I'm wrong, but the bank here was locally chartered, is that right?"

Two of the supervisors nodded. "We issued the charter ourselves," Jones added.

"It isn't a federal crime to steal from a locally chartered bank, gentlemen. Nor, for that matter, is murder a federal violation unless an employee or representative or ward of the United States government is the victim. As far as I know, none of those requirements was met in the bank robbery and resulting deaths this evening."

"But we need help," Bright said. He pointed toward young Frye. "We can't depend on him to recover our money, you know. And Lord only knows whether the bank carries insurance sufficient to cover our loss."

"It does not," Hightower said flatly. "I happen to be on the board of directors, Howard. Cash on hand in the vault rarely exceeds seven or eight thousand dollars at any given time. We, uh, chose to insure against loss up to . . . uh"— he looked embarrassed —"five thousand dollars."

"So between us we could be on the hook for nearly seventy thousand out of our own pockets, Vance?"

Hightower nodded unhappily.

"Jesus!" Bright blurted.

"And that is not a federal crime?" Jones asked.

"That's right, gentlemen. The way things stand right now, I can't do a thing here but look for my own federal escapees, Paul Markham and the woman known as Jessie."

"But with this declaration of emergency?"

"If you do that, gentlemen, and specifically request federal assistance on an emergency basis, I'll be able to take whatever steps are necessary to find my prisoners and your White Hoods."

"And recover our money as well?"

"Yes, sir."

Hightower frowned. "You say you shall be empowered to take unspecified but presumably necessary steps, Marshal. What, exactly, do you mean by that?"

Longarm smiled at the man. Hightower, it seemed, was stuffy but not stupid. He had picked up on that unspoken but very large point. "Things that I can almost guarantee you won't like at all, sir," Longarm admitted.

"Such as?"

"If you really want me to tell you, I will. But I think the voters around here might be happier with you three gentlemen if you can honestly plead ignorance." He grinned.

"After I'm gone, boys, I won't mind a bit if the folks around here cuss an' call me names. It might be better if you can point fingers at me and cuss right along with the rest of them."

This time Hightower smiled. "You are no stranger to the realities of political life, Marshal."

"No, sir, I'd have to admit that I am not."

"So you want us to pass this declaration of emergency and in effect write you a blank check to do as you wish in our community, is that it?" Bright asked.

"That is exactly what I'm asking, sir."

"And our alternative?" Jones asked.

Longarm shrugged. "You go your way and I go mine, gentlemen. I worry about finding Jessie and Paul Markham, while you and Charlie here hunt for the White Hoods and the missing money."

All three supervisors glanced toward their thoroughly cowed young deputy. Charlie Frye wasn't even old enough to shave on a regular basis, but he was all the local law that was left in Thunderbird Canyon now. Not that Markham and Mayes would have been any better, really, but Longarm refrained from saying so.

Hightower harrumphed and straightened his tie. He leaned forward and rapped his knuckles on the table. "Gentlemen, I call this emergency meeting of the Board of Supervisors to order. Do I hear a motion for approval of a Declaration of Emergency?"

"And a request for assistance from the United States Government," Longarm added.

"Yes, uh, and that too."

"So moved, " Jones said.

"Second," Bright added.

"Roll call vote, Mr. Secretary."

Bright was acting as secretary, Hightower apparently as president

"Bright. Aye. Jones?"

"Aye."

"Hightower?"

"Aye."

"The motion is carried, Mr. President."

"So ordered, Mr. Secretary."

"Thank you, gentlemen." Longarm stood. Lordy, but he was tired. But there was no help for that. Like the old saying went, he could catch up on his sleep next winter. Right now there was work to do.

Chapter 25

At 3:45 A.M. the three men representing the security forces of the three Thunderbird Canyon mines arrived. There was Phil Neal from the Huckman, Dan Sawyer for the Tyler, and a badly shaken Arnold Batson for the Arrabie. Batson's boss Jack Thomas had died in the explosion, and his second-in-command had not yet had time to get used to the idea that he was now in charge of things for the Arrabie. All three men had had to be pulled away from the rescue efforts still going on at the bank site.

"Thanks for coming, boys," Longarm told them.

"You better have a damn good reason for bringing us here," Neal said. "There's a chance somebody could still be alive under that shit."

"Of course there might be," Longarm said evenly, not believing it for a moment. "But you men being there won't make the difference. I need you here."

"You need? Who gives a fat crap what you need, mister?"

"It's Marshal, not mister, and as of thirty-five minutes ago, Mr. Neal, you care what I want. The county supervisors have declared a state of emergency, and as of now I'm in charge of this canyon and everything that happens in it. More particularly, I'm in charge of everything that goes *out* of it."

"You don't mind if we check up on what you say, do you?" Sawyer asked.

"Of course not." Longarm produced the signed proclamation Hightower had given him, and let each of the three inspect the document.

"All right," Sawyer said. Neal frowned but voiced no objection. Batson acted like he was in too much shock to care about much of anything else for the time being.

"I'm going to need your help," Longarm said.

"Rounding up the White Hoods?" Sawyer asked hopefully, and for the first time Batson's expression indicated some degree of interest in the conversation.

"If this involves throwing down on those fuckers," Batson said, "You can count on me and my crowd for anything we can do to help."

"And ours," Sawyer said.

Longarm looked at Neal and received a quick nod of agreement.

"I was hoping you'd feel that way about it,"

"We do," Sawyer assured him. "Aside from the money part of it, those were some pretty good boys who died in that explosion. We want those sons of bitches."

"So do I," Longarm told them. "I also want the former sheriff and the madam known as Jessie."

That brought a spurt of questions from the security men, none of whom had heard about the sheriff's arrest. Longarm had to explain it to them.

"Jesus," Neal whispered.

"Right. So while we're looking for the White Hoods, we're also looking for Markham and the woman. And the first thing I want done, before we waste another minute sitting here, is that I want a guard posted on the railroad tracks down where the canyon squeezes into those narrows. I want you to send two men from each mine, every man armed and equipped to stay a while. The orders are that no one, and I mean *no one* goes past them."

"That won't be so easy to do, Marshal. I mean, there's plenty of places a man can hide on a train. We can search the cars and the rods and what not, but, hell, a fella can burrow down into the ore or crawl inside the wood car and stack wood over himself . . . just lots of ways."

"I'll take care of that," Longarm told them. "What I want the guards to do is to make damn sure nobody passes them on foot."

"That we can do easy."

"If you boys can guarantee me that much, then I think we'll be able to get a handle on this thing."

"Marshal, you got my word on it anyhow."

"And mine."

Batson just nodded.

"Won't anybody walk out of here."

"Then I want you each to go get your people moving. Quick as you're done, come back and we'll talk some more about the rest of what I have in mind. Mind, though, nobody, not even one of the big bosses, goes out along those tracks."

"What about if you—"

"I won't," Longarm cut him off. "You can tell the guards that too. I won't be writing out any passes, and I won't be sending any messages. If anybody tries to tell them otherwise he's a liar and probably one of the White Hoods, and they have my permission to shoot if the liar resists. Understood? No exceptions, not even for county supervisors. Not for nobody."

"Guaranteed," Sawyer said. "Nobody goes out until this thing is over."

"And you are all sure that no one can leave any other way but by the tracks?"

"No chance, Marshal," Neal said.

"No chance," Batson agreed.

"Not even by foot?"

"I've done a lot of hiking and climbing around here, Marshal," Batson said. "It's kind of a hobby of mine. The way we're cut off back here I don't think a man could make it out afoot unless he had ropes and pitons and a hell of a lot of mountain climbing experience. Of course, in the areas you can reach, there's an awful lot of places a bunch like the White Hoods could crawl into and hide, for months if they had to while they waited for things to cool down."

Longarm smiled. "I think they're gonna find that once I get hot, I don't cool down so easy. Not until I get what I want, that is. And right now what I want are those White Hoods and the former sheriff."

"You don't get any argument from us on that one, Marshal."

"We'll go get our guards set, then come see you. Uh, would it be all right if we send more that two men per outfit? We could send a good sized crew and supplies to keep them there. Set up a rotating schedule with at least one man from each mine standing guard at all times?"

"That sounds all right to me."

"Then we'll see you shortly, Marshal. An' you'd better know that no son of a bitch will be leaving Thunderbird Canyon till those murdering cocksuckers are dead."

Longarm raised an eyebrow.

"Or in irons, of course," Sawyer said without conviction.

The man's meaning was clear enough. These men who had just lost friends in the bank explosion had no intention of letting a single White Hood live long enough to stand trial for his crimes.

"I'll see you after a while then," Longarm said. He forced himself to his feet again with a weary sigh and headed for the train depot while the security people hurried off into the night.

Chapter 26

"You want *what*?" The trainmaster planted his fists on his hips and glared.

"Oh, I don't think it's all that difficult to understand." Longarm struck a match and bent to the flame, lighting his cheroot. He shook the match out and flicked the spent stick into the cinders and gravel that lined the edge of the roadbed. "Think of it as a vacation," he said.

"You son of a bitch," the trainmaster declared.

"It's a common enough opinion," Longarm agreed pleasantly.

"I don't care what you say, mister..."

"It isn't mister, it's Marshal. And if you so much as make steam in that boiler until I say different, man, I'll have you in irons on charges of obstructing justice." Longarm smiled at the angry man. "With a nice, clean record behind you, I'd say you wouldn't get more than eighteen months, maybe two years out of it."

"You can't be serious," the trainmaster said in a voice that was more pleading than threatening now.

"Matter of fact, sir, I'm just about as serious as I can get. This train doesn't move, not an inch, until we've got a handle on the White Hoods."

"But that...you don't realize what that means," the trainmaster tried again.

"The way I understand it, stopping this train from moving means that Thunderbird Canyon is isolated. Completely cut off from the rest of the world. Nobody in,

114

nobody out. No food, no booze, no nothing until this matter is cleared."

"I can't believe you would stand there and tell me—"

"Of course you can't. You wouldn't do such a thing to folks. Well, I would. And I have. Anybody wants to complain, you just point the finger at me. I've been cussed before. I reckon I can stand it again. Anybody complains, you explain to 'em that you ain't responsible. But I suggest you keep in mind that no matter who complains or what they say or do or promise, if this train moves again before I say it moves again, it's you who'll be pulling time in a federal prison and not them." Longarm clamped the end of the cheroot between his teeth and smiled at the frustrated trainmaster.

"What am I supposed to tell Meade Park?" the man demanded.

"Tell 'em the truth, of course. I never get upset about anybody saying anything that's so."

"But . . ."

Longarm turned and walked over to the cab of the locomotive where a grime- and soot-covered fireman was feeding chunks of split pine into the box. He climbed the short steel ladder into the cab and tapped the man on the shoulder.

"Pull your fire," he instructed.

"What?"

"You heard me. Dump it."

"But we'll need—"

"Not today you won't."

The fireman looked past Longarm to the trainmaster and received a reluctant nod confirming the marshal's order. "Dump it, Johnny."

"If you say so, but damned if I unnerstand . . ." The fireman shook his head and muttered and cussed some, but he grabbed a poker and shovel off the rack nearby and began pulling the fire.

"Just to make sure nobody does anything funny," Longarm said, "as soon as that boiler cools some, I want the water drained, too."

"Shit, is there anything else you want? The keys t' my house maybe? My oldest daughter for a sacrifice?"

Longarm chuckled, even though that slight effort made his head feel like it was splitting apart. "Just keep this train sitting right where it is, and we won't have a problem."

He left the train crew to their unexpected morning efforts and headed back toward the hotel. It would be daylight soon, and already there was enough pale, predawn blush in the eastern sky that Longarm could see the small troop of shotgun-bearing security guards moving down the tracks, their arms laden with boxes of provisions and bundles that would likely be tents and bedding.

Thunderbird Canyon was closed off now, he realized with satisfaction. No one could enter the canyon. More imporantly, no one could leave it.

The White Hoods and Paul Markham were at this end of the canyon still, and here they would remain until Longarm had them safely in custody. Again in Markham's case. For the first time, though, as far as the infamous White Hoods were concerned.

He rubbed his eyes and felt the prickly growth of beard stubble on his chin. Right now he needed to see the security chiefs again and get them moving. Then perhaps he could steal an hour or two for some sleep before he got down to the down-and-dirty of the search for the murdering thieves who had dynamited the bank.

Lordy, but he did need some rest. He walked on toward the hotel with a shambling, stiff-legged gait that made him look and feel twenty years older than he was.

Chapter 27

Soft tapping on his door and a low, urgently repeated, "Marshal. Marshal Long?" brought him reluctantly awake. The knocking and the whispering continued.

He sat up, his head still aching from sleep promised but as yet unfulfilled, and rubbed his eyes.

"Marshal Long? Please, sir?"

The fool out there continued to whisper. Why the hell he would do that, Longarm couldn't figure. Was he afraid of waking Longarm or something? Hell, that was why he was here, wasn't it?

"Come in," Longarm groaned.

"Door's locked," the whisper came back.

"Oh." Longarm yawned, reached for a cheroot and shuffled slowly across the hotel room to the door.

He was beginning to think he'd have gotten more rest on this case if he'd set up his bed in the middle of a railroad station. Kansas City's, for instance. There would've been fewer visitors and passersby pestering him there.

The young man in the hallway looked apologetic but eager. "Good news, Marshal."

Longarm grunted and stepped aside to let the man in, then took his time about lighting his smoke. Good news right now would be about twenty uninterrupted hours of sleep. "What is it, uh . . . ?"

"Tim Blaisdell, sir. I work for Mr. Sawyer at the Tyler mine."

Longarm grunted again. He still felt half asleep.

"It's the White Hoods, sir."

Longarm blinked.

"We caught one of 'em, sir."

That cleared the last of the cobwebs. Longarm was fully awake now. Early morning sunlight was streaming through the single window in the hotel room, so he could not have slept long. After that news, though, he did not need more. "Tell me about it," he said, reaching for his hastily discarded clothing from the night—morning—hour or two—before.

Blaisdell was grinning now. "It was the boys down along the tracks that caught him, sir. Just where you posted 'em. This ol' fella came slipping along through the rocks just afore dawn. They hunkered down where they was . . . Bully Ryan, who's in charge down there, he thought they should set up kinda out o' sight, y' see . . . so they stayed where they was and let this fella come to them. An' he did. Walked right into 'em and throwed his hands high when he seen he was caught."

"And you're sure he is one of the White Hoods."

"Yes, sir," Blaisdell said with a grin and a bob of his head. "Had a hunnert dollars gold in his pockets an' a folded flour-sack hood stuffed in the same pocket, sir."

"A flour-sack hood?"

"Yes, sir," the grinning security guard affirmed. "Eye holes cut outa the cloth an' everything."

"Well I'll be damned," Longarm said. "Now wasn't that a piece of luck."

"Yes, sir. The whole plan worked just like you figured." Blaisdell looked about as pleased as a pup with a new kid to play with.

Longarm finished dressing and belted the Colt in place at his waist, then stamped his feet to settle them inside his boots. His damned socks felt clammy and moist, but he hadn't exactly had time to get laundry done lately. "Let's go meet this man with the white hood, Tim."

"Yes, sir." Blaisdell acted like this was about the most

exciting thing that had ever happened to him. And probably it was.

Longarm stopped downstairs in the hotel long enough to order a breakfast prepared and sent over to the jail—for himself, not the bastard with the hood in his pocket—then followed the guard to the courthouse.

The White Hood was a man in his twenties, large and heavily muscled and badly in need of both a shave and a bath. His nose showed signs of considerable battering in the past, and there were small scars laced over and through his eyebrows and on his cheekbones. A small-time prize-fighter somewhere in the past, Longarm concluded. And not a very good one at that to be so badly marked. This time, though, he himself was the prize, and his captors were congratulating themselves loudly.

"You haven't left the tracks unguarded, have you?" Longarm asked.

"No indeed. We got a full crew down there still."

"Good." Longarm gave the prisoner a thorough looking over through the bars of the cell door, then said, "The rest of you assigned down on the tracks can go back now. I'll handle this gentleman."

The guards looked disappointed, but they were still happy enough about their success that this would not keep them down for long. They gave a few last looks at the White Hood and left.

"Tim," Longarm said before Blaisdell disappeared in the hallways.

"Yes, sir?"

"If you would be so kind, Tim, stop at the hotel, please, and ask them to double that breakfast order for me."

"Yes, sir." Blaisdell thumped down the flight of narrow stairs, leaving Longarm alone with the prisoner.

The man looked apprehensive, as if he expected to be beaten now that there were no witnesses present. He sat on the flimsy cell cot with his back to the door and head hanging.

Longarm fingered through the things that had been

taken from the prisoner's pockets when they brought him in. There were the five gold double eagles Blaisdell mentioned, a handful of loose change amounting to eighty-three cents, a pocketknife with a badly nicked blade, and a bright pebble.

The pebble was rose quartz. It had a clear, clean tint of pink through the translucent stone, was not at all cloudy, and was a pretty thing even though it was of no actual value.

The hood that lay beside the other items was as Blaisdell had described—originally a sack intended to hold probably twenty pounds of flour. The cloth had not even been washed, and a dry, dusty powder of ground wheat clung to the corners where the sack had been sewed by machine. Eye holes had been hacked out of the cloth, and a drawstring intended to contain the flour remained in place where it could be tied loosely around a man's neck to keep the hood in place. A man wearing such a hood would be effectively concealed. The rig was simple but efficient.

Longarm tossed it back onto the desk and picked up the pebble. He crossed the small room to stand in front of the cell and extended a hand through the bars.

"I think this is yours?"

The prisoner looked at him with suspicion.

"A good-luck piece?"

The man shrugged.

"You can have it back if you want."

This time the man smiled. He came forward and took the bit of quartz from Longarm. He handled the pebble with a degree of tender concentration and pleasure that was surprising. Longarm got the impression that the prisoner felt much better now that he had the pebble in his possession again. There was something here that was slightly askew, not quite right, but Longarm could not nail it down.

"My name is Long," Longarm told him.

The prisoner smiled and nodded. He cupped the pebble in one palm and stroked the pretty stone with the fingers of his other hand.

"What's your name?"

"Donald James Potter," the prisoner said. His voice was . . . odd. Almost with a hollow sound to it.

The name meant nothing to Longarm. He was sure he had never seen it on any poster or wanted notices.

"Have you had breakfast, Donald?"

Potter shook his head. "I'm hungry."

"Me too. The hotel will send something over soon."

Potter grinned and looked about as happy as a bee in blue clover. Now that he had his pebble back and breakfast was on the way, Potter looked like he hadn't a care in the world.

Longarm cocked his head to the side and studied the man for a moment. Donald James Potter seemed poor pickings for a desperado.

"Tell me about yourself, Donald," Longarm suggested.

Potter shrugged and continued to admire the cool, pink depths of the quartz. He stroked it again and smiled.

"Well I'll be damned," Longarm said softly to himself. Potter ignored him, giving his full concentration to the stone in his hand.

Donald James Potter was simpleminded.

Was this how the leader of the White Hoods had been successful for so very long? By using carefully directed men with mush for brains who hadn't the wit or initiative to get out of line or give things away? Or for that matter, to demand more than what they were given?

It was a damned interesting thought, Longarm reflected.

But it might be something of a challenge trying to get hard information out of a man like this. Certainly bullying would just make the poor devil sull up like a cranky old steer. Bullying was something Donald James Potter would have had all too often in the past. Likely he would deal with it by simple withdrawal into himself. Perhaps, though, they could have a friendly chat over breakfast.

"Do you need anything, Donald?"

Potter shook his head. His hair was too-long uncut, and greasy from being long unwashed as well. If he had been

121

wearing a hat he must have lost it. He concentrated happily on the pretty stone in his palm.

Longarm shrugged and went to sit at the desk that once had belonged to Paul Markham while he waited for the breakfasts to be delivered.

Chapter 28

No man can exist as an invisible entity. Someone had to know something about Donald James Potter. How long he had been in Thunderbird Canyon. What he did here. Who he associated with. Someone had to have seen him, had to have had contact with him. Longarm had to find whoever that might be because unfortunately, poor Potter himself was incapable of giving that information.

Longarm did not believe Potter was lying to him or trying to hide anything. It was just that the poor soul had not the mental capacity to remember what he had for his last meal, much less any information that would help lead Longarm to the man or men who had put Potter up to the bombing of the bank, where men of the community had died during the night. Exactly how many men was still in doubt, as no one was yet sure if all the bodies had been recovered, and searchers were still hauling wreckage away from the ruins of the building.

It was something of a wonder, really, that Potter was able to recall anything about the affair, but the explosion had made some impression on the fuzz and fog that was his feeble brain.

He freely told Longarm what little he knew. There had been a loud, loud noise and a marvelous burst of flame. He'd found the bright flame in the night very pretty, apparently. Almost as pretty as his pebble. That was probably the reason he was able to recall something about having been there and seen it all. Potter dimly remembered something about a smaller flame too. He may have been the one to light the fuse that set off the explosion. He was not really sure about that, though.

Longarm shuddered when he thought about the dim, dark shadows that were Donald James Potter's thought processes. But there was nothing he could do to help the man nor, it seemed, to get much more in the way of information out of him.

He left Potter safely, and quite contentedly now, locked inside the jail cell and went out to see if anyone else in town could add to the little he knew about the White Hood prisoner.

The saloons and whorehouses would be his best bet for information, he suspected. Potter was earthy and direct in his appetites. If he had been in town any length of time at all he surely would have shown up in public somewhere.

"A half-wit named Potter, you say?" The barman shook his head. "No, I don't remember nobody like that lately. But say, Marshal, surely you ain't serious about stopping the train from running. I mean, I'm down to my next to last barrel of beer, Marshal, and I just can't . . ."

Longarm ignored the complaint and turned away. This was the third saloon he had visited, and so far the proprietors and employees of the town's drinking establishments seemed much more concerned about their own affairs than they were about being helpful, damn them.

He went back outside and tried the next place.

"Donald James Potter? Sure I know him. Good worker too, let me tell you, Marshal."

"You know him?"

"Jeez, I just said that, didn't I? He swamped for me here off an' on for, oh, three, four weeks it's been now. Showed up here one night all wore out and hungry . . . I think he walked in on the tracks 'cause he couldn't afford the price of a ticket . . . and I gave him a job. Sort of, anyhow. I mean, he didn't want much. But he'd come in here late 'most every night, and I'd feed him a dinner of whatever was handy, and after I'd close he'd sweep up an' empty the cuspidors an' like that, and I'd give him some nickels outa the till. Hard worker, Donald is. Had to be showed what was wanted every time, but once he got it straight what he was to do he'd stay at it until I told him to quit. Surely he ain't in any trouble, Marshal."

"Considerable trouble, I'm afraid," Longarm said.

The bartender frowned. "That's a shame now. I'm sorry t' hear it."

"Yeah. You say he's been here three or four weeks?"

"Something like that, but I wouldn't swear to it."

"You've been a big help."

"Yeah?" The bartender smiled. "Gee, Marshal, I'm glad."

"But I'm afraid you'll have to find a new swamper from now on."

"Or go back to doing it my own self, damnit. That's the way it usually works with the mines paying good wages to anybody with a strong back, damnit."

Longarm bought a half-dollar's worth of cheroots from the barman and was about to order a beer when Blaisdell came puffing through the door.

"Finally," the young security guard said. "I been looking for you, Marshal."

"What is it this time, Tim? Find another White Hood suspect?"

"No, sir, but we found Miss Jessie's body."

"Body?"

"Yes, sir." Blaisdell bent over and gulped for air.

"If she's dead, Tim, I expect she'll wait while you get your breath back. You want a beer or something?"

"No, sir. I don't drink."

The bartender winked at Longarm and uncorked a quart bottle of root beer. "Two?"

"One," Longarm told him.

The barman poured one root beer and one rootless variety for Longarm. Blaisdell gulped down his soft drink while Longarm sipped at his beer.

"Now tell me," Longarm said when Blaisdell had his wind back.

"That woman you was looking for, Marshal. One of the boys working in the sorting shack at the Arrabie found her. She was beat to death an' thrown on the tailings dump. The guy doing the sorting at the Arrabie seen her when he went to throw out some chunks of no-pay that were too big to go through the crusher. He tossed this one rock out the window, like, and seen it thump inta this woman laying right there on the slope. Shook him up bad, it did."

"She was already dead, though?"

"Yes, sir. We're sure about that 'cause she was cold as a trout when he ran down to see if he'd hurt her. I guess she'd been dead most o' the night for her to be so cooled off already."

"Has the body been moved?" Longarm asked.

"Yes, sir. Some of the boys from the Arrabie are bringing her down now. I come ahead to see if I could find you."

"Then I guess we'd better go take a look." Longarm drained off the last of his beer and paid for both drinks. "I might be back to ask some more about Potter," he told the barman.

"I'll be here, Marshal. If I happen to be sleepin' it's just upstairs, and somebody can fetch me down for you."

"All right, thanks."

Jessie's body was already being carried into the sawdust-packed icehouse when Longarm and Blaisdell got there. She was definitely not pretty to look at now. Blaisdell had said she was beaten to death, but Longarm was not prepared for the extent of damage that had been done to the once attractive woman. Her face was not recognizable as the woman Longarm had known, and only her hair and jewelry identified her.

She was no longer wearing the gown Longarm had last seen her in either. The fancy but fragile garment had been exchanged for a sturdy but plain riding habit, and she had

126

on a pair of tall, tightly laced logger's boots that looked to be several sizes too big for her.

"Was anything found with the body?" Longarm asked.

"What do you mean, Marshal?"

"Anything like a blanket roll or backpack. She's dressed for hiking, like she expected to be hiding out in the mountains. I'd think she would have carried some supplies with her and probably some bedding."

Blaisdell checked with the Arrabie guards who had brought the body down, but they all agreed that the only thing discarded on the tailings dump was Jessie's body itself. There had been no pack or bedroll.

Longarm rubbed his eyes and tried to get his fatigue-fogged thoughts in order. "You can go ahead and lay her out," he said. "Or have her buried, for that matter. I don't expect I need to see anymore here."

"You want us to show you where she was found?"

"No, I don't think that will be necessary. I expect I know who killed her and why."

Blaisdell and the other guards looked impressed, but Longarm was not in a mood to explain it to them. He would, of course, confirm his suspicions. He headed back up toward the whorehouse Jessie had operated.

Chapter 29

"Yes." The girl's accent made it come out sounding more like "Jess," but Longarm couldn't fault her for that. She had a good command of a language that was not her own, and that was more than he could say for himself with his few words and phrases of this or that tongue. "Miss Jessie and Sheriff Paul were here during the night," Rosalie said. "We were afraid. We hid, but they did not look for us."

"Do you know what they did when they were here? Where they went in the house?"

"Oh, yes. I show you?"

"Please."

She led the way past the bloodstains where Walter had died and into the office. The carpet had been ripped loose in a back corner of the room, and a barrel safe set into the floor was standing open. Longarm had not spotted the floor safe when he was here before, although it stood to reason that the madam and whoremaster must have had a place to keep their profits from a business Markham was not able to publicly acknowledge owning. The discovery was no great surprise.

Jessie's gown of the night before was discarded over a chair, along with her dainty shoes and flimsy, lace-trimmed underthings. There was no indication of what she would have taken for supplies and bedding, but Longarm was sure there would have been something.

So the two of them had grabbed the cash and fled. But Markham would have been figuring that a woman would slow him down, perhaps give him away in the mountains where he planned to hide. And of course the son of a bitch wouldn't have wanted to share the profits with a woman who was now a distinct liability to Paul Markham's future well-being.

So the shit would have killed her and kept the money all for himself. The man was a first-class prick. Longarm had to give him credit for that much anyway. When it came to making a son of a bitch of himself, Paul Markham didn't go in for half measures.

"They won't be back," Longarm assured Rosalie. "You and the other girls don't have anything to fear about that again."

"You are sure?"

"Yes."

"We don' know where to go now. Wha' to do."

"You can stay here, of course. Is there enough food in the place to last you a while?"

"Yes. Some food. Plenty whiskey."

"Just stay here, then, until I know if I'll need you to testify in court. After that I'll see if the government can't arrange to have you sent home."

Rosalie blushed. "I cannot go home again. Not after . . . you know. After the t'ings I have done." She had begun to cry, making no sound but with fat tears rolling down over her cheeks.

Longarm brushed them away with the bail of his thumb and lightly stroked her dusky cheek. "You didn't do anything bad, Rosalie. Bad things were done to you, but that wasn't your fault. Nobody back home ever has to know anything about those things. Not if you don't tell them." He smiled. "Besides, it isn't anything you have to decide about right now anyway. Think about it. Talk it over with the other girls. For the time being just keep the front door locked and the men out. They don't have to know anything either. If you need anything, come to me about it. Okay?"

It took a moment, but he got a smile and a nod out of her.

He left Rosalie and the other victims of Jessie and Markham and found Batson at the Arrabie offices. The man still had not gotten over the shock of Jack Thomas's death, but he was in much better shape than he had been during the wee hours before dawn.

"I take it you've heard about that woman's body being found on our tailings dump," Batson said.

"Yes, and I have a job for you and a couple of your people if you're up to it, Arnold."

"If it will bring us any closer to finding those men who murdered Jack, I am."

"Only indirectly," Longarm admitted. "I need this other business off my back so I can concentrate on the White Hoods. The reason I want your help in particular is that I believe you mentioned having done some hiking and climbing in the area. As a hobby, I think you said."

"That's right."

"Paul Markham is trying a run for it on foot, Batson."

"No place for him to run to," the security chief insisted.

"Apparently he thinks there is. Or at least thinks he can hide out long enough for things to cool off down here and allow him to slip out on a train eventually."

Batson snorted his disbelief about that.

"Markham is the man who murdered that woman. He's hiding somewhere up there with the money he was supposed to split with her from their slave trade. I expect wherever he's gone to ground, he started out from the whorehouse and climbed up past your tailings dump on his way to it. He stopped to beat his partner to death rather than have her slow him down. By now I'd guess he's found his hole and crawled into it."

Batson thought about that for a moment. "From town past the tailings side of our operation and then on up . . . yeah, I can think of a couple trails he might've taken. And some prospect holes and a few natural caves where he might think he could hide out if he's got supplies with him."

"He does," Longarm said.

Batson nodded. "I'll find the son of a bitch for you, Marshal."

"If you can take care of that, Arnold, I can handle the White Hoods and the recovery of the payroll money."

"No problem with my end of it, Marshal. I'll take a couple of boys with me, and we'll have him down in two days. Less'n that, maybe."

"Make sure your people are armed. Even a rabbit will fight if you corner it."

"I know just who t' take with me."

"Good." Longarm smiled. "Before you leave you might wanta stop at the jail and pick up a set of Markham's own handcuffs to haul him back in."

Batson smiled. "I'll do just that, Marshal."

Longarm left the Arrabie and walked down to the train depot where he found a still irate trainmaster and a bored-looking telegrapher in the office shanty.

"No," he told them, "I haven't changed my mind about allowing your damn train to run, so don't ask. But I do want to send a wire to my boss in Denver."

That news did not arouse any noticeable amount of pleasure with the railroad employees, but Longarm ignored them and wrote out the message he wanted sent to Billy Vail.

Time was entirely on his side now that the robber gang was bottled up at the head of Thunderbird Canyon, and for a change he had the luxury of calling in reinforcements no matter how long that might take.

Chapter 30

Anxiety knotted Henry's stomach like an acid-drenched fist as he paced the railroad platform at Meade Park.

He pulled his watch out and snapped the cover open once again. He had been doing it every two or three minutes since midmorning. Not that it did any good, of course. But he had to do something to alleviate the frustration he was feeling.

He wheeled and went back to the railroad office once again. He had been doing that every five or ten minutes, with no greater result than rechecking his watch.

"Try them again," he said.

"Marshal," the exasperated telegrapher groaned, "I just tried them ten minutes ago."

"I know you did. Now try them again."

"Yes, sir." The telegrapher rolled his eyes in a gesture of sorely tried patience. But he did as the bespectacled deputy demanded and once again bent to his key.

The man tapped out the transmission code, waited and tried again.

There was no response.

The line remained dead.

"I'm sorry, Marshal. Nothing."

"Damnit," Henry snapped.

He went back out onto the platform where the Meade Park town marshal and two deputies were waiting on a bench, obviously not nearly so concerned as Henry was.

"The downrun is half an hour overdue," Henry said.

"Thirty-four minutes," the town marshal agreed calmly.

"Something has happened up there, damnit, and I am afraid I know what it is. The White Hoods hit the train yesterday afternoon, and they've gotten away somehow."

"I keep trying to tell you, Marshal," the local lawman said patiently, "no matter what's happened up there, there's no way out except past us."

"But why is that wire dead? And why hasn't the train come down this morning? Can you tell me that?"

"Nope." The local took out a plug of tobacco and gnawed a corner off the disgusting looking thing. "Whatever the reason, though, there's nobody coming out without he goes past us. An' whenever that train does come down, we'll be right here waitin'."

"We could send a handcar up the tracks," Henry said for probably the tenth time.

And for probably the tenth time the local marshal explained with weary patience. "That jus' wouldn't be a good idear, Marshal. If the Thunderbird Run is comin' down when we're tryin' to go up, why, there's places where there ain't even anywhere to jump to. A man'd get squashed like a bug if he got caught on those tracks in a damn handcar. No sir, the best thing for us t' do is set right here an' wait. Something or somebody'll come down outa that canyon sooner or later. I figure t' be right here when they do."

"You have to at least send someone to guard the tracks where the narrows widen out and—"

"I already done that, Marshal. I told you that already."

"Oh. Yes, I suppose you did." Henry ran a hand over his face, removed his spectacles and wiped them clean, though they were not dirty, and began to pace back and forth along the platform again.

It was just so damnably *frustrating* having to wait like this and not *know* anything.

If only Longarm would show up, Henry would feel better. But apparently the messages sent to Snake Creek had missed him. Now there was no telling where he might be or how long it would take before he bothered reporting in and learned that he was needed here.

Damnit all anyhow, Henry thought unhappily.

He took out his watch and checked the time again. Three and a half minutes since the last time he had looked. He glared up the empty tracks toward Thunderbird Canyon and felt the bile churn inside his stomach.

What could *possibly* be happening up there?

He turned and strode once again toward the telegraph office. If he couldn't reach Thunderbird Canyon at least he could still communicate with Denver. Maybe Marshal Vail would have some thoughts about what he should do now. Henry was not honestly very hopeful about that, but the effort itself would give him a sense of purpose now, however temporary.

He did not believe he had *ever* felt so nervous before.

Chapter 31

Longarm woke and stretched. Three whole hours of sleep he had gotten. It felt like a considerable luxury, by damn. He was almost human again. Almost. He still had some catching up to do, but there would be time for that later. Right now the afternoon sun was partially obscured by the mountain peaks to the west, and it was time to see that his prisoner had supper.

He dressed quickly and went downstairs to order two dinners sent over to the jail, then snugged his Stetson into place and stepped outside.

The sun had disappeared now, but there would still be several hours of daylight remaining before the cool evening. The air felt good. Up the slopes to either side of the town the mines were in full operation despite the troubles of Thunderbird Canyon. The crushers thumped noisily inside the close confinement of the narrow canyon, the sound a low, dull, heavy thing that penetrated bone-deep and was felt more than heard.

The mining operations were modern and efficient, powered by steam and gravity, and capable of extracting and processing great quantities of raw silver ore daily. Already there was a stockpile of crushed material at the railroad hoppers. If the train continued to sit idle for very long the ore would be piled too deep, and the mines would likely have to suspend production until Longarm gave permission for the train to move again.

That, of course, was tough, but not something Longarm

was going to worry about. He had the White Hoods in a bottle now, and that immobile train was the cork that was keeping them confined.

In another few days—hell, four, five days, it didn't matter—Smiley and Dutch and the rest of the boys would be in Meade Park. As soon as Longarm got the signal that they were in position he would order a handcar for them, and the roundup could begin. In the meantime, if he was able to get a line on the gang himself, why, that would be all right too.

He was feeling pretty good as he stuck a cheroot between his teeth and ambled down the steep streets toward the courthouse.

He climbed the stairs to the top floor of the building and hung his hat on the rack by the door. Donald James Potter was dozing on his cot. He woke when Longarm came in and sat up blinking. He smiled happily at the tall deputy who had put him behind bars, obviously holding no grudge about it. Longarm suspected that the poor half-wit honestly did not realize the trouble he was in.

"Hullo," Potter said sleepily.

"Hello, Donald. Hungry?"

Potter spent several moments thinking about the question and forming an answer to it. Finally he nodded. "Hungry," he affirmed.

"Our supper will be here in a few minutes," Longarm said. "If you promise you won't try to run, Donald, you can come out here to eat."

Potter looked puzzled. "Run? For my supper?"

"Never mind." The man had no idea what he was talking about.

Longarm got the cell keys from the desk and unlocked the barred door so Potter could join him at the desk. Longarm tossed the keys back into the drawer and noticed again the few items that had been taken from Potter's pockets when he was captured. On an impulse Longarm pulled them out and placed them atop the desk. "Do you remember these, Donald?"

Potter looked at them carefully, then smiled. "My knife. An' my money."

"Who paid you the money, Donald?"

Potter shrugged. "A man."

"Do you remember his name, Donald?"

Another shrug.

"What about the hood, Donald?"

"Hood?"

"Sure. This." He pushed the flour-sack hood toward Potter.

"Tha's just a bit o' cloth, y' know. Hoods are black, Hangmens wear hoods." He shuddered. "I seen a hanging once. I 'member that good." He shuddered again.

Potter frowned for a moment, then his expression cleared as he put the memory of the hanging aside—something that seemed to come easy enough to him—and idly reached forward for the gleaming gold of the five double eagles.

His childlike mind seemed to be attracted to bright, pretty colors, and for several minutes he peered closely at the gold, fondled the coins, played with them. Longarm doubted that they held much value for him beyond their color and shininess, but he liked them well enough.

Footsteps sounded on the stairs beyond the jail door, and Longarm said, "Put those down now, Donald. I think our supper is here."

Potter smiled and did as he was told. He placed the coins into his palm one by one with slow, deliberate care to form a tiny valuable stack of minted gold. Then he picked up the white hood from the desk, and with infinite attention to what he was doing wrapped the coins inside the cloth and stuffed the small bundle into his pocket.

"Why did you do that, Donald?"

"Do what?"

"Wrap those coins like that."

Potter shrugged again. "I dunno. Keeps 'em nice, I guess."

"Oh."

Longarm leaned back in his chair and fingered his chin while he stared at the open, perfectly innocent expression of his prisoner. There was something. . . . He shook his head, to himself rather than for Potter's benefit, and looked up to greet the hotel waiter who had puffed his way to the top of the stairs with a heavy tray in his hands.

The aroma of tallow-fried steak filled the room when the towel was lifted from the plates, and Potter began to grin hugely.

"Me too," Longarm said.

Both men pitched into their meal with good appetite.

Chapter 32

Longarm tossed his napkin onto the greasy plate that was all that remained of an excellent meal and pushed his chair back. Potter had long since finished the last scrap of food available. The prisoner ate with an animallike speed and intensity, making loud slurping noises and using both hands to bring great bites to his face. A pleasant dining companion he was not.

"Time to go back to the cell, Donald."

Potter accepted the instruction without a trace of regret, pausing only to check once again and make sure there was nothing edible left on the tray. Then he stood and calmly headed for the lockup. He looked quite happy with the whole situation. Longarm got the cell keys from the desk drawer and followed.

"In you go, Donald."

Longarm reached for the cell door to swing it closed behind the prisoner. To his left there was the brittle sound of glass shattering. A lead slug spanged nastily against one of the steel cell bars, leaving a bright, shiny smear of fresh lead where a moment before there had been only paint, and sending fragments of soft lead whining through the room.

"Down!" Longarm barked.

He dropped to his belly, Colt in hand, as a second gunshot snapped through the broken window and again ricocheted dangerously off the cell bars.

Longarm fired blindly back into the new-fallen darkness. He had no target to aim at, no hope whatsoever that his slug would find a mark. He only wanted to give the sharpshooter pause.

A third incoming bullet tore splinters of wood out of the window frame and thumped into the wall behind Longarm.

"I don't like this," Potter complained. He was standing at the cell door with a blank, uncomprehending expression.

"Get down, Donald. Lie in your bunk. Stay there."

Potter nodded and walked slowly toward his cot. He lay on it and closed his eyes as if for a nap.

Jesus! Longarm thought.

A fourth bullet ripped through the window, higher this time, taking out what was left of the glass and spraying half the room with tiny shards.

Longarm felt one of them slice into his right cheek. Another nicked his ear. If this kept up . . .

He fired through the window into the darkness twice, his shots quickly thrown without aim, then rolled, came to his knees, and leaped toward the wall where the night lamp was burning. He didn't take time to blow the lamp out, just slashed sideways with the barrel of his Colt, smashing the bulbous globe and extinguishing the flame that was providing the sniper with light for his shooting.

The jail went dark, only a faint glow of light from the staircase landing seeping in through the half-open door now.

"Stay where you are," Longarm hissed.

There was no answer, and Longarm could not be sure Potter had heard. There was no time to worry about that now.

Another lead slug spanged off the jail bars. But this time Longarm was able to see the muzzle flash of the gunshot from the hillside facing the back of the courthouse.

Longarm fired twice toward the place where he had seen the flame, then spun away from the window and raced out of the jail and down the stairs, taking the steps two and three at a time and fumbling to reload as he ran.

If the gunman thought he was still trapped inside the jail . . .

He raced out into the night, ignoring a handful of confused, loud-talking men who were standing on the street corner pointing up the hill toward the source of the gunshots.

Elsewhere the men on the street were unalarmed, the noise of the crushers partially drowning the sound of the shots so that there was little commotion.

Longarm ran around to the back of the courthouse and began climbing the steep hillside. Another spear of flames and lead split the night far above him. Good. The gunman did not realize that he had suddenly become the hunted rather than the hunter.

Longarm ran past the pilings that supported the foundation of a house suspended over midair from a precariously thin purchase against the hard rock of the hillside. He ran beneath the house, emerged on the far side of it, and began climbing again.

Twice he tripped over loose stones or trash that had been discarded on the hillside. Once he sprawled forward, landing painfully on his chin and chest. He scrambled back onto his knees and drove himself upward, grabbing with his free hand for support whenever he could.

He was only halfway up to the level where the gunman had been, and already he was puffing for breath at the steepness of the climb and the altitude of this canyon head. If only the man was still there . . .

Another shot rang out overhead, and Longarm almost smiled. He was closer now but did not want to tip the ambusher with a shot that might miss. He needed to be closer still. Gulping for breath, his chest aching from the effort of it, he continued to climb as rapidly as he could force himself.

He was close enough to hear now as the gunman turned and began to run. Damnit, Longarm groaned to himself. With a burst of waning strength he threw himself upward, the last few feet until he reached a level section of trail or ledge.

The gunman was a dark, dimly-seen shape retreating up

the trail to Longarm's right. The town was beneath them now, its lights bright and its sounds gay in the night. Above, in the direction the trail led, there was only the dark, unlighted bulk of the mountains and the wild, empty lands beyond the mines.

Longarm raised his Colt and made an effort to control his breathing. His chest was heaving and heart pumping, and he knew the conditions were impossibly poor for accurate shooting. He aimed as carefully as he could, though, and squeezed gently on the trigger until the big .45 bucked and thundered, and his vision was blurred by the burst of muzzle flash in the night.

The footsteps of the fleeing gunman continued without faltering, and he was sure he had missed.

Doggedly, Longarm holstered the Colt to leave both hands free in case he fell. He set out at the swift, flowing lope of a long-distance runner, chasing not so much the gunman now as the diminishing sound of the man's footfalls as he retreated high into the mountains.

"Gotcha, you son of a bitch," Longarm panted into the darkness before him. Because with Longarm between him and the town, the gunman had nowhere to go now except to hell.

Chapter 33

Longarm stopped and leaned against a pillar of cold, jagged rock on the uphill side of the ledge. The ledge disappeared around the stone spire at this point as it curved sharply with the contour of the mountain. Beyond the turning would be a perfect place for an ambush.

He breathed deeply—easier now that the pain of exertion was subsiding in his chest. He drew the Colt again and replaced the one expended cartridge in the cylinder before, gun held ready, he edged forward once again. Speed was not a factor now. And a mistake could mean death.

He dropped into a crouch and shuffled forward on the ledge. Before him there was nothing but darkness. Behind him was the danger that he might be silhouetted against the glow of lamplight from the bustling mining town. Despite the danger, he kept his eyes down on the slender thread of rock ledge immediately under his feet. In darkness the hunter cannot trust his eyes. A shadow can turn suddenly into an imagined enemy. A rock can seem a charging grizzly so real the hunter would swear he can smell its breath. In darkness the hunter has to relie on his ears alone.

Longarm crept forward.

There was nothing ahead. Nothing at all he could hear except the faint soughing of the breeze winding its way past rocks and through the branches of an occasional juniper or cedar with its roots clinging to bare stone.

Longarm cursed softly to himself. The gunman had gained ground on him here. But he had had no choice. To go bursting fast and stubbornly around such bends would be perfectly safe every time but one. And that one unsafe time could be fatal. He jammed the Thunderer back into its leather and pressed forward.

The ledge they were following was probably a game trail, but no human had ever improved it. It widened and narrowed without plan or pattern, sloped down toward a dizzying drop here, then leveled out as smooth and wide as a city road not a handful of rods further up.

The gunman had to be somewhere ahead of him on the trail, though. There was nowhere else for him to go. Not unless he was willing to climb up or down, and in the darkness it would not be possible for anyone to do that without dislodging the loose stones on the steep hillside. Longarm would certainly hear if the gunman tried to leave the trail and make his way up the slope or down it.

A sliver of moonglow appeared to the southeast, and Longarm smiled silently to himself. As soon as the moon broke free of the peaks there would be light enough for him to make up lost time on the ambusher. A thought came to him as he moved cautiously through the night.

He hadn't ever had time to lock Donald James Potter into his cell. The man was free for the moment if he chose to be, and he had the hood and gold coins still in his pocket. For a prisoner, poor Donald could have himself quite a night of it until Longarm got back. Still, the halfwit had nowhere to go. Not any more than the White Hoods did. He could run, but he couldn't hide. He would be back in custody soon enough. Longarm was not worried about Potter.

For that matter, he realized, he would not have been worried about Potter anyway. The man hadn't sense enough to think up trouble on his own. If anything, Longarm rather liked the simple fellow—his eating habits aside—and felt regret about having to jail him. Potter was no threat to anyone in Thunderbird Canyon.

The man ahead on this trail was another story entirely. A man who would shoot from ambush out of the night was a menace. Why he would do that was not secret, of course. Longarm was the one who was keeping the train from running. With the federal deputy dead, the mine owners would want the train moving again as quickly as possibly. And there would be a hundred hiding places available once that train moved. So Longarm's life was in danger until the rest of Billy Vail's boys got here. Or until the rest of the White Hoods were behind bars. It was as simple as that.

Longarm stopped and cursed under his breath again.

The ledge continued on in the direction it had been following, but here a game trail angled off above it.

He was high on the mountain now, well above timberline. Up at this elevation a game trail would have been carved over hundreds of years by bighorn sheep or possibly by the shaggy white goats that somehow made their living high above the levels where the runtiest, hardiest of trees could survive.

The question now was whether the gunman had stayed with the ledge or moved onto the trail. And whether the gunman knew this country well.

Longarm made his decision. A White Hood, come here within the past month or so as Donald Potter seemed to have done, would almost certainly have little or no knowledge of the high country surrounding the mining camp. The gunman therefore almost certainly would have followed the trail instead of the ledge. Longarm's reasoning was simple enough. And he had to assume that the gunman would reach the same conclusion. A natural ledge can peter out without warning at any time, or any whim of nature. A game trail, on the other hand, *has to go somewhere*. So, Longarm decided, a sensible ambusher trying to get away in unknown country would naturally choose to follow the game trail instead of the ledge.

Longarm's fingers brushed briefly but reassuringly over the grips of his Colt. Then, slowly, careful of his footing, he began to mount the trail carved here by countless hard hoofs. He had to be closing on the son of a bitch now. Had to be.

Chapter 34

"Marshal? Wake up, Marshal, please."

Henry's eyes opened, gummy with too much sleep that was not at all restful, and he sat up. He had been sitting at the Meade Park town marshal's desk when he drifted off, and he had slept badly, with his mouth open so that now it was annoyingly dry. He licked his lips with a tongue that held no moisture and swallowed several times, trying to work up some saliva.

"What is it? The train? Did you get through finally?"

"Whoa, Marshal." the deputy said patiently. "There's a message for you, that's all."

"A message. Thank goodness." Henry jumped up, reaching for his derby and adjusting his spectacles, but the deputy stopped him.

"It ain't a message from Thunderbird," the man said. "Sorry, but we still haven't been able to raise anybody up there."

"But if it isn't . . . ?"

"It's from your boss in Denver," the local deputy said.

"Oh." The momentary excitement faded, and Henry felt the anxiety return.

Whatever could be happening up there? He was all too fearful already that he knew what was happening—had happened—at the other end of the useless narrow-gauge rails. That was what was worrying him, damnit.

Henry left the small office and turned down the block toward the railroad depot. It was dark. He had no idea what time it was or how long he had been sleeping, but there was a feel in the air of late night. Meade Park seemed to have gone to bed, leaving only a few lights showing in private homes and in the hotel. One of the two saloons in town had even closed for the night. Unlike a mining community, which Meade Park no longer really was, the town closed its doors early.

There were no night lamps burning on the railroad platform at this hour, but light showed at the windows of the telegrapher's office. Henry had prevailed on the man to stay at his post overnight, sleeping on a cot beside his sending key if he had to, so there would be no possibility of a message from Thunderbird Canyon being missed.

Frankly, Henry was having visions of an entire town under siege. Many explanations were possible, of course. Nearly all of them involved mayhem and destruction in one form or another.

He shivered in the cool night air and tugged the lapels of his coat close over his chest.

The telegrapher greeted him pleasantly enough when he entered the office.

"For you, Marshal." The man handed him a single sheet of paper with the message scratched out in a spidery hand.

WHAT IS STATUS THERE QUERY HAS LONG RE-
PORTED YET QUERY AM SENDING REQUEST AD-
DITIONAL INFORMATION FROM STONE VIA
JOHNSTON COMMA FORT SMITH STOP ALSO DIS-
PATCHING ADDITIONAL DEPUTIES YOUR ASSIS-
TANCE STOP VAIL

Henry felt relief wash through him at the thought that the regular deputies were on their way. And apparently Billy Vail had gotten through to Longarm also or there would not have been that question about him showing up.

Thank goodness. He would not have to face the White Hoods alone.

"I need to send a reply." he told the telegraph operator.

147

"Write it out now if you want to, Marshal, but we gotta relay through Soda Springs to get down to the Union Pacific an' the Western Union operators. There's no night man on at Soda Springs now. He signed off twenty, thirty minutes ago. So whatever you send, it won't go out till tomorra morning when he comes on again. Me, I'd like to go home now too, Marshal."

"You'll stay right here," Henry snapped forcefully. "You shall keep this key open regardless."

"Yes, sir," the operator said with a weary sigh.

"And I shall wait until morning to write out my answer. Perhaps by then we will have heard something from Thunderbird Canyon."

"Yes, sir," the operator said with absolutely no belief in his voice.

"If anything does come in . . ."

"I'll find you." the operator said in a bored tone.

"Right." Henry snapped the brim of his derby, spun on his heels, and marched back out onto the street feeling much better now than he had earlier.

Longarm and Smiley and Dutch should be here soon. Already he was feeling less alone.

Chapter 35

Longarm shivered and cursed. The damned game trail went somewhere, all right. It led to a rock slide that had swept the whole damned thing away.

There was a gap of thirty or forty feet between the part of the trail he was on and the place where the trail resumed on the other side of the break. The trail was clearly visible in the moonlight. There just was no way to get to it from here. The trail carved by generations of wild sheep and goats had been wiped completely out by the rock slide.

Longarm stood and peered up and down the mountainside. There was no sight of the gunman he had been chasing, and in both directions the mountainside was barren except for loose scree. There was no place the man could have hidden. There was no way he could have gotten across the treacherously loose rock left in the wake of the slide. *He was not up here.*

With some more muttered cussing, Longarm turned and began retracing his steps along the abandoned game trail. He had been climbing the trail more than an hour, but he had had to move with slow caution then on the assumption that the gunman was somewhere just ahead of him. Now he hurried, trying to get back down to the ledge before the man realized that Longarm was no longer behind him and tried to double back to the safety of the town where he could lose himself in the crowd.

Longarm had never gotten a look at the son of a bitch. The man could stand next to him at a bar and Longarm would never know it. Not if the fellow reached Thunderbird Canyon.

Longarm stretched out his strides, moving as fast as he dared on the narrow trail, now and then dislodging a stone that went tumbling over the lip and clattering down the mountainside. There was no help for that, though. He had to hurry or risk losing the man.

He reached the place where the trail and ledge met in little better than half an hour. Without hesitation he turned onto the ledge in the direction he had originally been following. If he had missed the gunman—if the man had already realized that he was free to head back to town—there was nothing Longarm could do about it now.

The only chance Longarm had to catch him was the hope that the gunman was still somewhere ahead of him on the ledge or wherever it led.

Very far ahead of him.

Or free and laughing behind him.

Bitter at the thought of his own miscalculation, Longarm hurried on.

Chapter 36

"You sure look like shit this morning, Marshal," young Frye said. Longarm met him at the courthouse steps as the local deputy was coming outside.

"I'm entitled to look like shit, Charlie. I had quite a night, and I feel like shit too."

Frye grinned, obviously unaware of the previous night's excitement. "Say, Marshal, you didn't bust the window in the jail, did you?"

Longarm glared at him. "No damnit, I did not break your window."

"I was just asking. Jeez. No need to get touchy about it. I mean, I asked that fella in the cell, but he couldn't tell me nothing."

"Potter?"

Frye shrugged. "Yeah, I guess that's his name. You know, the dummy."

"He's still in his cell?"

"Sure. I was just up there. I was going to get his breakfast now. You want me to bring you something too?"

"Please. And, Charlie?"

"Yeah, Marshal."

"I'm sorry if I snapped at you. It's just that I've been hiking up in the damn mountains all night long, and I expect I'm feeling kinda bearish now."

Frye gave him an uncomprehending look, and Longarm realized there was no point in pursuing his frustrations with the youngster. "Look, I appreciate your offer of that breakfast. I really do. Thanks."

"Sure thing, Marshal. I'll have 'em sent right up. One for you an' one for the prisoner." He turned and walked toward the business district.

At least that was one thing that had gone all right. He didn't have to go hunt for Donald James Potter again.

Longarm felt of his chin. He needed a shave, but tired as he was after hunting through the mountains the entire night he would likely cut his own damn throat if he tried to shave before he got some rest. And it would take a little while before the breakfasts were delivered. While he was waiting he could see if there was any response yet from Billy Vail.

He walked down to the railroad depot. The platform was deserted, but some workmen from the mines were hauling crushed ore down ready for shipment for processing. The hoppers were full already after missing only a single day's shipping schedule. Soon the owners and managers at the mines would be squawking about that.

The telegraph operator was at his desk. His work went on regardless of what the mines and the railroad might do, Longarm realized.

"Good morning," Longarm said in as civil a greeting as he could manage.

"Nothing good about it," the operator said. He looked like he too had had a rough night, although probably his would have been in the pursuit of pleasure instead of a sneak with a rifle.

"If you say so," Longarm said with a grin. The telegraph operator's eyes were so red and puffy that the sight of the man almost made Longarm feel fresh just from the comparison. On the other hand, Longarm hadn't had a chance to look in a mirror. Maybe he looked as bad, heaven forbid.

"Something I can do for you, Marshal?"

"I wanted to see if there's been a reply to the telegram I sent yesterday."

"Sorry, Marshal. Not a thing for you. Just the usual stuff for the mines."

"Okay, thanks."

Longarm turned to leave, but the operator stopped him.

"It probably isn't my place to be saying anything, Marshal, but you might wanta know. The county supervisors are getting plenty unhappy about you not letting the train run. That train is awful important to us."

"So were those dead men and all that missing money," Longarm said coldly.

"Like I said, it probably wasn't my place to speak up anyhow. I just thought you should know."

"Yeah. Thanks."

Longarm left the telegraph office with yet another worry. If the mine-owning county supervisors decided to withdraw their declaration of emergency and their request for federal intervention in Thunderbird Canyon, what the hell would his legal position be?

He honestly was not sure if he could stay on the case after that or not. A judge who had six months to study law on a subject—any subject—and a whole damned army of lawyers telling him what he should rule about it, well, there just was never any way of telling what a ruling would come out to be. A deputy in the field didn't have that kind of time or expert help either one. All he could do was what he thought was right. And then half the time see his judgment shot to pieces after the fact. It was a bitch, Longarm thought, any way you looked at it.

Still, a good meal and a few hours of rest would put a better light on things. Assuming the ambusher from the night before kept to himself for a spell, that is.

Lordy, but he didn't think he had *ever* been on a case before that kept him so ass-dragging tired.

Chapter 37

Longarm woke in midafternoon to a rapping on his hotel room door. He didn't mind. Hell, he was getting used to it. And at least this time he'd gotten several hours of solid sleep. Anything over fifteen minutes was beginning to seem a luxury, and there wasn't anything wrong with him now that twenty hours or so of uninterrupted sleep couldn't cure.

"I'm coming." He pulled on his trousers and crossed the room barefoot—the place had not been swept since he checked in, and the floor was cold and gritty underfoot—to unlock the door.

He did not know the man in the hallway, but he was unarmed and seemed inoffensive enough. Longarm pointed the muzzle of the Colt down toward the floor and let him in.

"Sorry t' bother you, Marshal."

"No problem."

"I'm a loader at the Arrabie, Marshal. Morris, Jim Morris." He stood with his hat in his hand and bobbed his head. "Mr. Batson asked me t' run ahead and tell you they're comin' in now."

"They have Markham?"

"Yes, sir. That's exactly what I'm s'posed t' tell you, sir. Mr. Batson an' two other fellas. They're bringin' him down now."

"Alive?"

"I wouldn't know about that, sir, but I seen that they're

154

havin' to carry him. If he ain't dead he's at least shot up some."

"Thank you, Jim. Tell them I'll meet them at the courthouse."

"Yes, sir." Morris bobbed his head again and backed toward the door, tugging his hat on and in a hurry to complete this chore.

Frankly, Longarm did not particularly give a damn if Paul Markham was brought in living or otherwise. It startled him to realize it, and he reflected on it as he dressed.

Markham was a sick, venal, mean, and petty son of a bitch, and the thought of the former sheriff was disgusting to Longarm. But in truth the man's sins were minor compared with the murders of perhaps half a dozen men in the bank explosion, and the loss of more than seventy thousand dollars of uninsured cash. Longarm simply did not care if Markham died here or lived out the rest of his days in a federal prison. The kind of man who would force unwilling girls into short lives of pain and anguish was not deserving of consideration beyond the minimum required by duty and decency.

Longarm finished dressing, felt of his chin and decided not to take time for a shave. He went down to the street and toward the courthouse in time to meet Arnold Batson and two of his men struggling down the steep hillside with a makeshift litter.

Paul Markham was in the litter. Longarm did have to look twice to determine that the one-time sheriff of Thunderbird Canyon was quite thoroughly dead. He had been torn apart by numerous gunshots fired at close range.

"You think you shot him enough, Arnold?" Longarm asked sarcastically. He was beginning to wonder if sending Batson to find the fugitive had been such a good idea after all.

"What? Oh." Batson frowned.

Now that he was paying attention to the living rather than the dead, Longarm could see that the security man was pale and looked about half sick.

"We . . . uh . . . got kinda excited, I guess." Batson admitted.

"Tell me about it."

The men carrying the litter with Markham's body on it set their burden down. All three, Batson and both his helpers, looked haggard and unhappy.

"We cornered him easy enough," Batson said. "I mean, a man that don't know this country's pretty much got no place to go, Marshal, like I told you before. Take a wrong trail, and you won't get anywhere. For that matter, take the right trails and there ain't but so far you can go. So we were onto him pretty easy." He paused. "Say, d'you have a smoke we could share? We run out this morning while we were trying to get him down here."

"Sure." Longarm handed cheroots to each of the three and lighted one for himself as well.

"Thanks. Anyway, like I started to tell you, we got onto him real easy. He seen us coming . . . no way to avoid that up above timberline where we was . . . and he went to ground in a prospect hole on the north face of Mount Norman. Had a good field o' fire down the only trail we could use to get to him, and he had a revolver to hold us off with. Didn't get any of us as you c'n see, but he scared hell outa us a few times and sprayed Johnny there with some rock chips. So we had a kind of standoff for a while.

"Paul knew he was cornered, o'course. There wasn't any way for us to shag him outa there, but there wasn't anyplace for him to go neither. I remembered that hole, and it wasn't but forty, fifty feet deep into the rock. An' even if he'd got out of there, the trail he'd been on only went another couple hundred yards up the mountain an' petered out at another prospect hole."

Longarm drew on his cheroot and nodded.

"So anyway, after a bit he hollered out that he wanted to talk. Johnny stayed back in the rocks out o' sight, and Lew and me walked up to where we could talk." Batson smiled without humor.

"Turned out the son of a bitch wanted to try and buy his

way out. He said he had eleven thousand dollars cash on him, and he'd share it with us if we made out that we couldn't find him. Not that I know where he thought he'd go if we did turn back, but he gave it a try. Started out offering to give us half an' ended up trying to give us all of it if we'd just pretend we never found him." A grimace showed what Batson thought about that. "As if we could be bought. You know?"

Longarm muttered something and waited for the man to continue.

"Anyway, Marshal, I expect there's some folks as can be bought and some as can't. I'm proud to say that these fellas with me are the can't-be kind. We listened, an' then we tried to talk him out of his hole. At one point he even came out in plain sight, right there in front of us, an' showed us a wad o' cash money. Folding stuff, you see. Shoved his pistol down behind his belt and held the money out for us to look at, like that would tempt us more or something.

"Well, it didn't. And then I guess I did something stupid. I mean, prob'ly you would known how to handle it better if you'd been there, but I up and told him that me and my boys weren't for sale and that we were placing him under arrest."

It was becoming clear from Batson's expression and from the beads of sweat that were showing on his forehead that this was a painful recollection for him. "You did the right thing," Longarm assured the man.

"Thanks." Batson hemmed and hawed for a moment, staring down toward his scuffed, dusty boots instead of looking Longarm in the eyes now. "Maybe I did wrong, Marshal, but I was concentrating on telling him that we'd not hurt him and that he was under arrest and all like that, and I guess I just didn't pay close enough attention or something. Anyway, he ups and drops the money. Just opened his hand and turned loose of it. And naturally me and Lew looked at all that wad of money fluttering in the wind. And Markham, he hauls out his pistol and fires. Fired point-blank right into my face he did."

Batson pushed the hair back from his left temple and displayed an ear that was red and some stubble of hair that had been singed by fire. "Damn close," Batson said calmly enough, "but I guess he was excited then as we was, and the powder flash got me but the bullet missed. Got my attention, let me tell you. Scared shit outa all of us. But then me and Lew got untracked and grabbed for our guns, and Johnny started shooting and . . . we just kept shooting. It was awful, Marshal. I mean, none of us ever shot at a human person before, much less ever kilt anybody, and I guess we was scared and nervous, and we kept on shooting even when we didn't have to anymore."

Batson looked embarrassed. "I know I emptied my gun at him and then kept on cocking an' pulling the trigger even after the thing was empty, until Lew took me by the shoulder and got me to realizing what I was doing. I . . . I'm sorry about not being able to bring our prisoner in for you, Marshal."

"You did fine, Arnold," Longarm said. He meant it, "I couldn't have done any better myself."

"I feel awful dumb, though, trying to shoot an empty gun like that and being so scared I hardly knew what was going on or anything."

Longarm smiled and squeezed the man's shoulder. "You're probably too young to've been in the war, but I know a lot of soldiers then got so shook up in the fighting that they never fired at all, or if they did just shot into the air. Why, they used to go out on the battlefields when everything was over and recover all the rifles that'd been dropped. They tell that a lot of them, not just a few, but an awful lot of them, would be full to the muzzle with unfired charges. The soldiers would be so excited they'd never remember to pull their triggers. They'd load, throw the guns to their shoulders, then take them down and load again without ever shooting. Or they might shoot off the first round an' then never remember to load again during a whole battle. Yet they'd go right on fighting, and if you asked them afterward they'd honestly believe they'd been shooting the whole time. They really never knew different. Believe me, you boys did just fine."

"You really mean that, Marshal?"

"Yes, I do."

"Thanks. I guess. But let me tell you, Marshal, this business of shooting people just ain't for me. I . . . I got sick afterward. It isn't something I'd ever want to do again. I just don't know that I could. For sure not as a regular thing."

"Killing is ugly, Arnold. Sometimes, though, it's necessary. You boys did the right thing."

Lordy, how long had it been since *he* got sick after having to shoot someone? Too long, that was how long it had been. In a way, that was a damned shame. He didn't want to take human life lightly, damnit.

But the fact was that seeing men die, and taking lives, became easier with experience. In a manner of speaking, Longarm actually envied Arnold Batson his innocence and his reverence for life. When the time had come, though, Batson had done what he had to do. And perhaps that more than anything else was the measure of a good man.

Batson brightened a little. "We brought the money back, Marshal. I think we got all of it. It counts up to near sixteen thousand." He smiled a little. "Even when he was trying to bribe us, the son of a bitch was holding back plenty for himself."

Longarm laughed. Greed was something a man could count on, by damn. It was seldom possible to overestimate the power of greed in a man. Even when he was faced with the end like a rat caught in a corner and was bargaining for his life, Paul Markham stayed greedy.

On the other hand, Arnold Batson and his boys hadn't been swayed by the offer of a bribe of $11,000, and they wouldn't have been any more tempted by $16,000, Longarm felt sure. Some men are just plain straight and decent, and that was a good thing to remember.

Batson could have tried to pretend that Markham was empty-handed when he was caught—which Longarm would not have believed, but Batson would not have known that—or could have kept most of the money and turned in a few thousand.

Longarm had no doubt at all, though, that the men were proud to turn over every penny they recovered. What it came down to, he supposed, was that their pride and self worth were more valuable to them than $16,000. And there probably wasn't one of them who would ever see more than $50 per month pay in their entire lives. There were some real assholes in Thunderbird Canyon. But there were also some mighty fine people here, and Longarm was facing three of them.

"We'd've been back sooner," Batson was saying, "except for having to chase down some of that currency from outa the rocks and then having so much trouble getting the litter fixed up and hauling the, uh, the body back down."

"Nobody could've done any better than you did," Longarm said. "If you don't mind, I'd appreciate it if you'd take Markham's body the rest of the way down to the icehouse, and then you can meet me at the hotel. I think the government owes you the best steak in town at the least. I'd be proud to set it up for you."

"Thanks, Marshal, but if it's all the same t' you, sir, what I want more'n anything right now is to go home an' take a hot bath and a shave an' just . . . be by myself a while. We talked about that some. I think Lew and Johnny feel the same way. We don't want nothing out o' this but to try and forget it ever happened. If you wouldn't mind, sir."

"Mind? No, I certainly don't mind. You have my thanks, though, if that's all you will accept. Maybe later we can get those steaks."

"Yes, sir," Batson said politely. Somehow, though, Longarm knew there would not be a later. These boys were heartsick over having killed someone, even a shit like Paul Markham who was trying to kill them, and what they genuinely wanted now was to put the experience behind them and resume lives just as dull and ordinary as possible.

The three of them picked up Markham's body and struggled off toward the ice-house with it, and Longarm turned away. They were good men, he reflected.

And that was one problem that was off his back now. Paul Markham and Jessie were both dead now, and there would be no case to take before a federal judge on behalf of those Mexican girls waiting uncertain of their own futures at the whorehouse.

It occurred to him that something would have to be done with the money Batson had recovered from Markham. It belonged to no one, really. Longarm smiled and thought again about the captive, unwilling whores. He suspected he would be able to find something to do with that cash. Meanwhile, he still had to do something about the White Hoods.

As he walked back toward the hotel and a belated lunch, though, for some reason he kept thinking about Paul Markham and his capture. There was something in that that was nagging at him, and he couldn't quite put his finger on what it was. Oddly enough, he had the impression that it had little or nothing to do with Markham and Jessie. But he just couldn't quite drag it out to where he could look at it. He chewed on the thought while he walked.

Chapter 38

Longarm jerked upright in his chair and slapped his fork down beside his plate.

"Of course, damnit," he said aloud. "But *who*?"

He laughed, the sound abrupt and loud in the near silence of the restaurant.

Two men having a late lunch at the next table gave him a look that said they thought he was daft, but Longarm didn't care at all.

That was what had been gnawing at him ever since Arnold Batson told him about running Markham to ground.

It all fit now.

The failure of the White Hoods to show on Friday afternoon.

The explosion in the bank.

The fact that no one but poor, half-witted Donald Potter tried to leave town Saturday morning.

Even, by damn, the flour-sack hood found in Potter's pocket.

Longarm smiled to himself, thinking about the way Potter had had no idea that the flour sack even *was* a hood. When Longarm handed the article to him, Potter took it and used it to wrap around the coins for safekeeping.

That was the whole bugaboo with this search for the White Hood Gang. *There were no White Hoods!* Not, at least, in Thunderbird Canyon.

His thoughts were coming together now, and Longarm was becoming excited at the process of discovery.

The ambusher who had tried to kill him the other night. . . . No wonder the man wanted Longarm out of the way. He desperately needed to get the train running again. So he could make his escape with the stolen payroll money. Hell yes, he did. With the train running—whether Longarm was alive or dead—the law would be looking for strangers trying to escape in hiding. But the man who planned the payroll robbery would be a familiar face, right there in plain sight among people who thought he was a decent member of a decent community. The son of a bitch would be able to board the train and wander off to Meade Park in full view of everyone. No one would be inspecting baggage for the stolen money. They would all be looking for the sinister and unfamiliar members of the White Hood Gang.

Longarm almost admired the simplicity of it.

And when Longarm thought the man was trapped on the mountainside following the attack out of the night, he had been *right* about thinking a stranger to the country would follow a game trail before a ledge.

The thing was, the gunman was no stranger to this country. He had *known* where the trail and the ledge alike would lead and was shrewd enough to figure Longarm for sensible reasoning on the subject. That was exactly why he was able to stay on the ledge and give the slip to his pursuit.

Someone local, right here in town the whole time, had set this whole deal up.

The White Hood warning was a complete hoax, start to finish, just to force the authorities—Longarm right along with them—into doing exactly what the thief planned. And that was to keep all the payroll and royalty monies in one juicy lump, ripe for the taking, under guard but all together and available to a thief smart enough and brash enough—and vicious enough—to go after it.

Longarm pushed his plate away. His steak was only half eaten, but all of a sudden he was much too wound up to

163

care about food. He dropped a coin onto the table beside his neglected meal and hurried out into the sunlight.

He knew part of it. He was convinced of that now. But he still needed to fill in the rest of the picture.

He thought he had a pretty fair idea of how to go about that.

Chapter 39

His first stop was the obvious one. He took the courthouse stairs two at a time. There was a chance, just the barest chance, that under the proper questioning Donald Potter might remember enough to give Longarm a clue to the identity of the thief and murderer of Thunderbird Canyon.

Because Longarm was convinced now that Potter was guilty of nothing more, really, than having been a tool used by the murderer. Potter was hired as window dressing—paid a hundred dollars and told to try and sneak out of the canyon by way of the railroad tracks.

When the poor man was caught, as he inevitably would be, the hood in his pocket would "prove" that the White Hood Gang was behind the explosion and robbery.

And for a while Longarm had bought it, damnit.

No longer. Now Longarm cussed himself for not noticing before that the flour-sack hood taken from Potter's pocket still had remnants of wheat flour in the seams, *but there was no trace of the substance in the man's hair*. Potter had never worn the hood, and in fact had not even known that he was carrying something fashioned into a hood.

If he had noticed that to begin with it would have started the doubts and this train of thought that much earlier, damnit. Being dead beat and dragging was scant excuse for that failure, but there was no point in worrying about it now.

The important thing was that now he could talk to Potter not about the White Hoods and a crime that he had had nothing to do with, but about the things that *really* might have happened that night.

Longarm was wearing a grim smile when he reached the top floor of the courthouse building and hustled into the jail.

The smile was wiped away by what he found there.

The door to Potter's cell stood open, the keys still dangling in the lock. Donald James Potter was there. In the cell. Lying on the hard cot where Longarm had last seen him. The grass-stuffed mattress ticking was a dark and ominous red from drying blood, and the blood covered most of the upper part of Potter's body as well.

Longarm cursed bitterly and made sure there was no one else in the place, then entered the cell with regret.

Potter lay on his back with his eyes wide and unseeing. He had been stabbed and slashed repeatedly. One hand was clutching something. Hoping Potter might have grabbed at his attacker and snatched some sort of clue from the killer, Longarm bent to the pale body and pried open the cold, stiff fist.

The only thing Potter had, perhaps the one thing that had given him comfort in his life, was the rose quartz pebble the poor fellow had been so fond of touching and stroking and playing with.

Longarm felt anger rise then.

The poor bastard had been harmless. He probably smiled at the man who murdered him, just as he had smiled at the man who put him behind bars. Donald James Potter had not had the brains or the guile to hate or to fear, either one.

Somehow Longarm found this murder even uglier than those of the innocent men who had died in the explosion at the small bank.

The murder meant, though, that the killer was getting worried. Longarm was still alive, the train remained immobile on the rails, and time was on the side of the law. The killer wanted out, and he was becoming worried about the delays Longarm caused.

Gently Longarm replaced the pink pebble in Donald Potter's cold hand, and as gently pulled the dead man's eyelids closed. There was nothing more Longarm could do for Potter, except to find his killer, and unlike Arnold Batson, Custis Long was no stranger to death.

He turned and went back down the steps, although more slowly this time.

"No, sir, I haven't noticed anybody going up there," the county clerk told him. "But then, I mean, I wouldn't. You know? Guys go up an' down all day. I don't pay them any mind."

"Thanks." It was not a surprising response. It was the same one he had gotten from everyone on the lower floors of the courthouse. No one paid attention to anyone else. Particularly to people they would recognize as familiar faces on the streets of Thunderbird Canyon. And it certainly was no stranger Longarm was looking for here.

He tried the last office in the building with a similar lack of success and then moved outside.

He walked to the bank building. The debris left behind by the explosion Friday night had been cleared away now, leaving only the remnants of the ground flooring and a gaping hold down into the cellar.

The last of the workmen had gone, and the rubble of stone and wood that once had been a building was piled to one side. Some of the timbers and most of the shaped stone building blocks would be useful again. Even as Longarm watched, a man pulled a small wagon close to the trash heap and began picking through the stones, selecting some of the smallest and most uniformly shaped and putting them into the wagon for his own purposes.

"You couldn't tell me where the workmen have gone, could you?" Longarm asked.

"Not really, but I hear that most of the work was done by a crew from the Tyler. You could ask up there."

"All right, thanks."

167

It was a long climb to the Tyler mine, and Longarm was puffing by the time he got there.

The man who had been in charge of the rescue and clearing efforts was a shift foreman named Simmonds. Longarm found him in the small boardinghouse reserved for security and management people. Longarm hoped Simmonds was off duty because by midafternoon he had already been drinking heavily.

Longarm introduced himself and explained what he needed to know. "I was hoping you might have found something that would help," he said.

Simmonds grunted and reached for a refill, not bothering to offer a drink. From the way the foreman was going at it, Longarm suspected Simmonds did not want to let any of that bottle—or possibly the next one either—escape him.

"I'll tell you wha' we foun'," Simmonds said in a slurred voice. "A stinkin' mess is wha' we found." He grimaced and took another drink. "Wasn't nobody lef' alive in there. Couldna been." His face twisted and he looked like he might weep at the memory of the things he had seen in the remains of the bank building.

"How many—" Longarm began, but Simmonds cut him off.

"I don't *know*. Jesus God, man, tha's the thing. We don' even know fer sure how many died. They was . . . they was tore up so awful . . . we think . . . we think there's six dead. But Jesus God, we ain't even fer sure about that. It could . . . it could be five. Could be seven. We ain't even sure about that." He reached for the bottle again.

"You didn't find any money, though? There was nothing in the vault when you got to it?"

That was one of the things that was tugging at Longarm's instincts now. The payroll money, more than $70,000 and all of it in minted gold coin, was one hell of a bulky, weighty haul. It would take either time or a great deal of manpower for someone to move it.

168

The way this thing looked to be working out so far, the thief or thieves were short on manpower. One man, or anyway, no more than a few. More than that would not be able to keep the plan secret in a small, enclosed community like Thunderbird Canyon. The more people you have to trust to keep any secret, the less likely that secret will be kept. So he had to believe that the spurious "White Hood Gang" of Thunderbird Canyon was at most a handful of men.

Yet it would take time for a few men to move that much gold into hiding. They certainly had not had such an amount of time available to them *after* the explosion and virtual collapse of the bank.

Besides, the shattering force of the explosion dropped tons and tons of rubble onto the vault. The empty vault. If the explosion had been for the purpose of opening the vault, as Longarm and everyone else had been assuming right along, not stopping to think as Longarm was now, it would not have been possible for the thieves to reach the vault under all that stone and timber.

The gold had to have been stolen before the explosion.

Why in the *hell* hadn't he seen that earlier, Longarm moaned silently to himself.

The answer to that one was simple enough, of course. It was because he and everybody else was being led around by the nose in this thing, with the thief or thieves doing the leading.

The bank and vault were blown up and the vault was emptied, and therefore the explosion was to open the vault. That's what it looked like on the surface, anyway. And never once had anybody gotten around to questioning that obvious but erroneous "fact."

Well, Longarm was damn sure questioning it now.

That money was stolen before the explosion. Therefore the explosion itself was a ruse. A way of throwing the law off the scent.

Why, then, the deaths of five or six or seven good men? Obviously, Longarm realized, those men were killed in cold, deliberate blood to keep anyone from discovering the identity of the thieves.

Had the guards all been held under gunpoint while the heavy gold was transferred out of the bank, then placed near the vault and deliberately murdered with a heavy charge of dynamite?

That seemed entirely possible.

The men had to be destroyed to protect their murderer, just as Donald James Potter was destroyed.

Why with dynamite, though, damnit?

Why with all that noise and destruction?

Potter was knifed.

The murderer tried to kill Longarm with a rifle.

So why were the men guarding the bank killed in such a way that the attention of the entire town was immediately and dramatically drawn to the scene of the crime?

That, damnit, made no sense. Not on the surface of things, anyway.

The guards could have been tied and gagged and conveniently murdered by stabbing or strangulation so that the killers would have had hours to get away from the scene.

That made much more sense than the roaring devastation of a massive explosion powerful enough to rip a whole building apart.

"Was any of those men, those bodies, tied up, Mr. Simmonds? Did you find any ropes on their hands or anything like that?"

"What're you, some kinda fuckin' crazy?" Simmonds took another long swallow of the whiskey, although he looked like it was not giving him anything close to the mind-numbing relief he wanted.

Longarm decided to take the answer as a no. Simmonds or somebody would surely have brought it to his attention if that had been the case, anyway.

"Thanks," Longarm said. "You've been more help than you know."

Simmonds grunted and reached for his bottle. "There was friends o' mine in there, mister. Friends o' mine. An' I hadta pick 'em up in pieces." The burly mine foreman started to cry over his whiskey. "I reached for a hand, mister, an' that's all there was there. Just the hand. An' I don't even know whose it was."

Longarm left Simmonds to his misery.

Chapter 40

It was getting on toward late afternoon by the time Longarm got down the mountain to the town again, and the damned train was making steam. He went charging down to the depot ready to have someone's ass, but the trainmaster quickly explained.

"I'm not going anywhere, Marshal. Really. Just having my engineer run a check on the boiler while we got the down time." The man contrived to look and sound as innocent as a newborn. "Honest. We don't even have the cars filled. Look for yourself."

Longarm did and grunted an acknowledgment that the man was telling him the truth. "All right then, but see that you don't turn a wheel until I give you the go-ahead."

"I won't." The trainmaster pulled a plug from his pocket, offered it to Longarm, and bit off a chew for himself. "While you're handy, though, Marshal, would you mind telling me if this is gonna take much longer?"

"I don't think so," Longarm said. "Maybe you can make your regular run tomorrow morning."

The man looked relieved. "That's good news, Marshal. We stay down much longer and I'm afraid the line will start dockin' our pay." He grinned. "Deep as I'm in debt already, I couldn't afford that."

"Did I hear you say the train can run again tomorrow?"

Longarm turned. The telegraph operator had come up behind them and asked the question.

"It's only a possibility. I don't want you putting that on the wire, though. It all depends."

The telegrapher looked disappointed.

"While I'm here," Longarm said, "I'd like my answer from Marshal Vail."

"What answer?"

"To that message I sent him . . . when was it . . . yesterday?"

"Oh." The telegrapher shrugged. "Hasn't been no answer for you yet, Marshal. When it comes in, you want me to have it sent to the hotel or have somebody look for you personal?"

Longarm frowned, then relaxed. "Just have it sent to the hotel. That will be fine."

"Soon as it comes in," the operator said.

Longarm turned as if to leave, then stopped and said, "There's something I'd like you to do for me. It's important."

The telegrapher's lips twitched, hovering between a frown and an uncertain smile. "What's that?"

"I want you to find Deputy Charlie Frye and bring him here."

"Me, Marshal?"

Longarm's expression hardened. In a voice of stern command he snapped, "Yes, you, damnit."

"I'm supposed to be on duty, Marshal, right by my key, and—"

"Now!" Longarm ordered.

The telegrapher took a half step backward, then nodded and turned to hurry off toward the town.

"Kind of hard on him, weren't you?" the trainmaster observed. He rolled his cud from one cheek to the other and spat, expertly splattering a small spider that was climbing from the roadbed onto the platform.

"Maybe," Longarm conceded. "Easily ordered around, is he?"

"Who, Carter? I suppose so. Never thought about it before, but I guess you could say that."

"Yeah, well..." Longarm left the trainmaster and crossed the platform to the empty office. The telegrapher's key sat idle and quiet on the counter beside his desk.

Longarm glanced out the window to make sure the operator was not yet returning, then sat before the man's key.

U.S. Marshal Billy Vail had never taken this long to respond to one of his deputies's requests for assistance before. And Longarm did not believe Billy had gotten suddenly lazy now.

Longarm flexed his fingers for a moment, then bent to the telegraph key, tapping out a quick dot-and-dash series of letters.

A minute or so later he tried it again.

There was no response from the other end of the wire.

Longarm smiled grimly to himself, left the desk and began to poke around the railroad office.

When the telegrapher returned with Charlie Frye in tow, Longarm was relaxing in a swivel chair with cheroot cocked at a jaunty angle in his jaw.

"I have a job for you that I think the local law should handle, Charlie," he said.

"Yes, sir?"

Longarm removed the cheroot from between his teeth and aimed it at the telegraph operator's chest. "What I want you to do, Charlie," Longarm said pleasantly, "is to place that scummy son of a bitch under arrest on eight counts of murder and"—he grinned—"we'll add more to it shortly."

The telegrapher went pale. Charlie Frye blinked in confusion.

"Go ahead and try to run for it if you want," Longarm told the operator calmly. "I won't shoot you in the back. In the knees, but not the back. And it won't bother me a lick."

The telegrapher began to shiver. A dark, damp stain spread over the front of his trousers as he wet himself.

Chapter 41

The telegrapher's name was Jamison Carter, and he did not give the impression of being a particularly brave individual. Longarm had Frye cuff him and take him up to the jail where Donald Potter's body still lay untended. Frye got quite a start out of seeing it.

"You can take care of that later," Longarm told him. "Right now I want you to go downstairs to the next landing. I want you to stay on those steps and not let anybody up here. Nobody, you understand me?"

Frye nodded, though he was still staring at the dead man in the cell.

"No matter what you hear from up here, I don't want you or anybody else coming up those stairs, Deputy. I don't want any witnesses, you understand, and I'm making you responsible for that."

"Uh . . . yessir." Frye said dubiously. "I won't let nobody up until you tell me."

"Not even the county supervisors." Longarm said. "Nobody."

"No, sir. Nobody."

"That's good. Now, do you have any spare handcuffs?"

"We got some in the bottom of that cabinet over there."

"Good. Take your set and one of those extras and cuff Mr. Carter here to the bars with both hands so that he's kind of spread-eagled on his feet."

Frye looked like he could not believe what he was being told to do, but he did it. He got out a set of spare handcuffs

175

and a key for them. "Do you, uh, want him facing out or in, Marshal?"

"I want him facing into the cell so he can look at Potter while . . . uh . . . while I'm talking to him."

Carter looked like he might faint. For that matter, Charlie Frye did not look very far from it himself.

"And while you're switching that first set of cuffs from his wrist to the bars, Charlie, have the prisoner take off his shirt, would you, please?"

"Yes, sir."

Carter was shaking so bad the trembling could be seen from all the way across the room.

Longarm reached for another cheroot and took his time about lighting it.

"Downstairs now, Charlie. And remember, I don't want anybody coming up here to bother me, no matter what you hear. Anybody wants to complain about the noise, I'll take it up with them after. All right?"

Charlie Frye looked damned glad to be able to leave the room and rush down the stairs.

Jamison Carter was facing away, pinioned to the steel bars by the handcuffs on his wrists. He could not see Longarm. But he could imagine much. That, in fact, was what Longarm was counting on.

Longarm took a comfortable seat in the chair that had belonged to the now-dead—there seemed to be a lot of that going around Thunderbird Canyon lately—Paul Markham and took a pull on his smoke.

"Want to tell me all about it, Carter?" he asked in a low, mild voice.

"I . . . I don't know anything to tell you, Marshal."

"Uh-huh," Longarm said. "For instance, you don't know why the battery for your telegraph wire has been disabled or how it could be that no one in Meade Park has received any traffic from here in several days?"

"I . . ." Carter shook his head, but with a gesture that was more nervous than stubborn.

"It might interest you to know that I reconnected the battery. We have communication with Meade Park again."

"I don't know anything about that."

"You don't know anything either, I suppose, about why the operator in Meade Park never received any of the messages I told you to send. You remember. The ones you told me you did send."

Carter's knees sagged.

"Before we get down to the good parts of this interrogation, Carter, it's probably only fair to tell you that I've got most of this figured out by now. Including whose orders you've been taking. What did he promise you, Carter? Five thousand? Ten?"

"I never killed anybody, Marshal. I swear to God I never," Carter blubbered.

"He might believe you, Carter, but I damn sure don't. Your boss in this couldn't have killed Donald Potter. You're the one who did that. And you were a part of the bank murders too. It really doesn't matter who actually lit the fuse, you know. But you don't have to take my word for that. The judge will tell you the same thing. Before he hangs you."

"Oh, God, Marshal, I can't hang. I . . . I couldn't stand that."

"You'll manage," Longarm assured him. "Unless some judge is damn fool enough to let you off with just a prison sentence. Like if you were to cooperate and help me find your boss and the money." Longarm chuckled. "Except that I don't need your help, Carter. The money is in the bank basement. I can find it all by myself."

Carter began trying to wrench his hands free of the steel handcuffs, jerking from side to side so that the steel bracelets bit into his flesh. He began to moan and soiled himself again.

Longarm stood and slipped up behind Carter so he was immediately behind the man's ear. "Where is he?" he roared.

Carter jumped so hard he fell and for a moment was

hanging by his wrists. Longarm took a fistful of hair and hauled him back onto his feet.

"Where?" Longarm demanded.

"He . . . he'll kill me if I tell you."

"A judge will kill you if you don't. Tell me and I might, just might, keep him separate from you when I haul your ass off to prison. Keep it to yourself, Carter, and when I do find him, man, I'll tell him it was you who told me where to look."

"God, Marshal, you can't *do* this to me," Carter wailed.

"Oh, but I can," Longarm said calmly. "If you don't mind a suggestion, though, I think it's a little late to be thinking about God. I expect He's pretty disappointed in you by now. Now are you going to tell me or not?"

"Yes," Carter sobbed. "I'll tell you where to find him."

Longarm listened patiently while Jamison Carter blubbered out everything he knew and probably somewhat more. Only then did the angry deputy release the creepy weasel from the handcuffs and shove him into a cell.

"Frye!" Longarm bellowed down the staircase. "Go get Arnold Batson. Tell him to bring some of his people and meet me here on the double."

Young Frye looked confused again. He had been expecting screams and all he heard was some crying and babble from upstairs. But he did as he was told.

Chapter 42

Batson motioned for them to stop, then leaned closer to Longarm. "That's it, Marshal. The Pearly Number Two. You can see from the size of it that they never got far developing it. Low grade ore and getting worse as they went in, so they quit before they had even more money sunk in it and wasted. There's probably not more'n a half mile of tunnel in there."

He made that sound like it wasn't much, although to Longarm a half mile of digging through solid rock was one hell of a lot. Still, he knew that an active, established mine could have literally miles of tunnels and shafts underground.

Longarm frowned and tried to get a better look at the area. It was dark, somewhere past nine o'clock, and the moon was obscured by cloud cover.

The mouth of what once was the Pearly Number two yawned dark against the mountainside. Some regular shapes laid out on the ground would have been where buildings once stood, but their wood had long since been carried away and put to other uses. Now there was only a more or less level clearing in front of the tunnel. And damned few places where a man could take cover if it came to a gunfight. Longarm hoped he could resolve it without that, though.

"If we try and go in now," Longarm whispered, "we'd only be silhouetted against the sky. A man inside there could pick us off without hardly working up a sweat. I think we'd better lay up nice and easy until three, four o'clock in the morning. He should be asleep then for sure. He's got no reason to be expecting a visit. So we'll lay low for now, and when I think it's safe I'll go in by myself and see if I can't have a gun to his head when he wakes up."

"I think I should be the one to go in, Marshal," Batson said grimly, and Longarm was reminded anew that Arnold Batson was one decent man. He hated killing, as he proved with Paul Markham, but he was willing to put himself on the line again now when he believed it was his duty to do so.

"No, Arnold, this is my job. I'll handle it. I want you and your people to stay out here on the ready just in case I trip over a bucket or something and give myself away."

"I still think—"

"No. And that's the end of it. Just to be safe, though, I want you to send two of your boys over to that side of the tunnel and put the third man up over the top of it. Cartridges chambered but keep the rifles uncocked. We don't want any accidents, and we sure don't want to alert him that we're out here waiting for him."

Batson hesitated for only a moment, then nodded. He crept back to where the Arrabie guards were waiting and whispered to them. One moved silently forward toward the tunnel opening while the other two started across the clearing.

Without warning a rifle shot rang out of the tunnel, splitting the darkness with its flame, and one of Batson's men dropped his Winchester clattering to the ground and fell, grabbing his leg.

The other guard turned, snatched his fallen companion up, and ran with him toward the far side of the clearing as two more shots spat out of the tunnel toward them.

Longarm returned the fire, emptying his Colt into the mouth of the tunnel without aim, but in the hope that a ricochet might find a mark in there.

He reloaded, not at all minding that neither Batson nor any of the three guards had returned the murderer's fire. It

180

would be damned difficult for them if they had to, and he hoped he would be able to avoid the need for it still.

Batson, though, took a deep breath, aimed in the direction of the dark tunnel mouth, and fired.

"It's all right, Arnold," Longarm said, in a normal voice now that they had been discovered. "I'll do any of that that's necessary."

Batson nodded. There was enough light from the sky that Longarm could see the pain that was in his expression. Batson took his Winchester down from his shoulder. "Thanks."

Longarm moved forward, keeping to the side of the tunnel as well as he was able, and shouted, "Jack. Jack Thomas! You have nowhere to run, Jack. It's over. Put your gun down and come out now."

"Is that you, Longarm?" The voice sounded slightly hollow as it emerged from the enclosing rock, but Thomas sounded cheerful enough.

"It's me, Jack," Longarm called.

"I'll be go to hell. How'd you find me?"

"It wasn't that hard once I got it figured out, Jack."

There was a slight pause. Longarm suspected the Arrabie security chief was changing position inside the tunnel. "I sure thought I had it covered, Longarm. What'd I do wrong?"

"You stole a bunch of money and killed a bunch of people, Jack."

"Aw, come on, Longarm. You know what I mean." The voice did not sound quite so hollow now. Longarm was sure Thomas was moving closer to the mouth.

"Yeah, I know what you mean, Jack. You want me to tell you how clever you are?"

"No. I really want to know how I fucked up. Aside from doing it to begin with, that is.'

Longarm eased down until he was lying on his belly with the Thunderer stuck out in front of him and held ready. "It was the explosion more than anything, Jack," he shouted.

"What do you mean?"

"It wasn't so hard to work out that it had to be some-body local behind it since there weren't really any White Hoods. Hell, they're too smart to get themselves bottled up in a canyon with only one way out. So I worked on that some, but I got to admit I had trouble spotting you for the one behind it. After you got yourself killed and all."

The sound of Thomas's laughter drifted out of the tunnel.

"Like I said, Jack, it was really the explosion that tipped me to it. It didn't make sense. Killing all those people that particular way. And I happen to know how hard it is to really blow a human body into pieces. That's a damned unusual thing, Jack. Pretty much had to be deliberate. And an awful big charge of dynamite. So I got to thinking about that. Like how even in a mining camp just any-old-body would excite some interest if he wanted to buy that much explosive without any obvious need for it. And how hard it is to steal dynamite from a mine. Then it occurred to me how it was you, Jack, that suggested we keep all the money together so we could guard it overnight and not distribute it until morning.

"Not that I thought anything about that when you were dead, Jack. But then when I got to wondering why any-body would want to blow those men up, Jack, it occurred to me that maybe those two things were connected. And maybe you weren't quite as dead as everybody thought.

"And of course you didn't have much support in the guts or brains department in that partner you picked. Carter couldn't tell me everything fast enough once I got him started."

"Yeah, that son of a bitch. I needed him, though. Needed him to get that fake telegram sent so everybody'd blame the White Hoods and I could get it to fall into place." Thomas's voice sounded quite close to the front now, and Longarm took a fresh grip on his Colt and read-ied himself. He was betting that Thomas would count on his untried guards to hold their fire against a friend—the same friend, of course, who had blown several other friends to bits—and try to take Longarm and make a break for it.

"Actually," Longarm said, "you could have taken a trip out of the canyon and bribed some other operator to send your phony message."

There was a pause, then a sound of laughter. "Shit, Longarm, I never thought of that. That would've been better, wouldn't it?"

"Naw, I'd've nailed your butt anyway, Jack."

"I don't know, Longarm," Thomas called.

"I do," Longarm said softly to himself.

"I guess we have a standoff here, Longarm."

"I guess we do, Jack."

"What say we try and negotiate this, Longarm? I have seventy-two thousand dollars in here with me."

Longarm could hear Arnold Batson stirring behind him. The second attempt to bribe him in as many days would likely be having him pretty thoroughly pissed off, Longarm suspected. It just could be that Jack Thomas was counting more on a former friendship than Arnold Batson would be willing to deliver.

"Bullshit," Longarm said. "The money was hidden in the basement of the bank. I figure you had it transferred down there by the same fellas you killed. What'd you do, tell them that would hide it and keep it even safer?"

"Yeah, but . . ."

"I'm not bluffing you, Jack. You hid it in the steamer trunk behind the file cabinets in the southest corner of the place. It's already been found, counted, and turned over to the proper owners."

"You son of a. . . . Never mind that now, Longarm. I still think we can negotia—"

He came out of the tunnel hard and fast, driving forward in a rolling fall, a Winchester held in his hands, its muzzle sweeping at belly level toward the place Longarm's voice had been coming from.

Thomas's finger tightened on the trigger, and the Winchester spat lead through the air where Longarm would have been if he had been standing upright.

Longarm took his time for careful aim and was surprised to see Jack Thomas's head jerk backward a fraction of a second before Longarm fired to send a second, but unnecessary, bullet into the man's brain.

Behind Longarm, Arnold Batson sagged to his knees and began throwing up.

Batson, whose loyalties lay with duty and pride rather than with the turncoat Jack Thomas, had killed again.

Longarm got to his feet and went forward to verify that Thomas was no threat any longer. Then he turned back to Batson.

"Come along, Arnold. We have to get your injured man down the mountain." He smiled. "By the time we get there, I expect Marshal Vail and Henry will've made that handcart ride. If I have anything to say about it, man, the marshal will see to it that you get whatever commendation or rewards or whatever that the government can talk those three mines into."

Batson wiped his mouth with the back of his hand and shook his head. "I don't want—"

"I know," Longarm said. "But you've done the right thing, and it will look better to you in the morning. Come on, now." Longarm had to help Batson upright and half support him back down the trail while the other guards assisted the wounded man.

Watch for

LONGARM AND THE UTAH KILLERS

one hundred and twelfth novel in the bold
LONGARM series from Jove

coming in April!

LONGARM

Explore the exciting Old West with
one of the men who made it wild!

LONGARM

Explore the exciting Old West with
one of the men who made it wild!